W9-COM-386

**ROSA LIKSOM** is a Finnish artist and the author of over a dozen books. She won the Finlandia Prize in 2011 for *Compartment No. 6*, now translated into thirteen languages.

# ROSA LIKSOM

# COMPARTMENT NO. 6

Translated by Lola Rogers

Serpent's Tail gratefully acknowledges the financial assistance of
FILI – Finnish Literature Exchange

# FILI

FINNISH LITERATURE EXCHANGE

This book has been selected to receive financial assistance from English PEN's 'PEN
Translates!' programme supported by Arts Council England. English PEN exists to promote
literature and its understanding, uphold writers' freedoms around the world, campaign
against the persecution and imprisonment of writers for stating their views, and promote
the friendly co-operation of writers and free exchange of ideas. *www.englishpen.org*

  Supported using public funding by
**ARTS COUNCIL
ENGLAND**

Passages from Vsevolod Garshin's *The Scarlet Flower* translated by E. L. Voynich

A complete catalogue record for this book can
be obtained from the British Library on request

The right of Rosa Liksom to be identified as the author of this work has been asserted
by her in accordance with the Copyright, Designs and Patents Act 1988

Copyright © 2011 Rosa Liksom
Published by agreement with the Hedland Literary Agency
Translation copyright © 2014 by Lola Rogers

The characters and events in this book are fictitious. Any similarity to real
persons, dead or alive, is coincidental and not intended by the author.

All rights reserved. No part of this book may be reproduced, stored in a retrieval system
or transmitted in any form or by any means, electronic, mechanical, photocopying,
recording or otherwise, without the prior permission of the publisher.

First published as *Hytti Nro. 6,* by WSOY, Helsinki in 2011

First published in 2014 by Serpent's Tail,
an imprint of Profile Books Ltd
3A Exmouth House
Pine Street
London ECIR OJH
*www.serpentstail.com*

ISBN 978 1 84668 927 7
eISBN 978 1 84765 923 1

Designed and typeset in Garamond by MacGuru Ltd *info@macguru.org.uk*
Printed and bound in Italy by L.E.G.O. S.p.A., Lavis (TN)

1 3 5 7 9 10 8 6 4 2

thank you
gospodin / graždanin X.X.

MOSCOW HUNKERED DOWN into a dry, frozen March evening, sheltering itself from the touch of an icy sun setting red. The girl boarded the last sleeping car at the tail end of the train, found her cabin – compartment number six – and took a deep breath. There were four bunks, the higher two folded against the wall above. There was a small table between the beds with a white tablecloth and a faded pink paper carnation in a plastic vase. The shelf at the head of the beds was full of large, clumsily tied parcels. She shoved the unprepossessing old suitcase that Zahar had given her into the metal storage space under the hard, narrow bunk and threw her small backpack on the bed. When the station bell rang for the first time she went to stand at the window in the passageway. She breathed in the smell of the train: iron, coal dust, smells left by dozens of cities and thousands of people. Travellers and the people with them pushed past her, lugging bags and packages. She touched the cold window and looked at the platform. This train would take her to villages of exiles, across the open and closed cities of Siberia to the capital of Mongolia, Ulan Bator.

When the station bell rang the second time she saw a muscular, cauliflower-eared man in a black working-man's quilted jacket and a white ermine hat and with him a beautiful, dark-haired woman and her teenage son, keeping close to his mother. The woman and the boy said goodbye to the man and walked arm in arm back towards the station. The man stared at the ground, turned his back to the icy wind, pinched a Belamorka, lifted it to his lips and lit it, smoked greedily for a moment, stubbed the cigarette out on the sole of his shoe, and stood there, shivering. When the station bell rang for the third time, he jumped on the train. The girl watched him walk towards the back of the car with swinging steps and hoped he wasn't coming to her compartment. She hoped in vain.

After a moment's hesitation she went into the compartment and sat on her own bunk across from the man, who radiated cold. Both were silent. The man stared sullenly at the girl, the girl at the paper carnations, uncertain. As the train jerked into motion Shostakovich's Eighth String Quartet burst forth from loud, plastic loudspeakers in the compartment and passageway.

And so the Moscow winter, the steel-blue city warmed by the evening sun, is left behind. Moscow – the city lights and the noise of traffic, the circle dance of churches, the teenage boy and the beautiful dark-haired woman with one side of her face swollen – are all left behind. The sparse neon signs against a morose, pitch-black sky, the ruby stars on the towers of the Kremlin, the waxed bodies of the good Lenin and the bad Stalin, and Mitka, are left behind. Red Square and the Lenin Mausoleum, the lacy iron railings of the spiral staircase at the GUM department store, the Intourist international hotel with its foreign currency bar, its floor staff commandeering living space in the cleaning cupboards and looking for Western make-up, perfume, and electric razors, are left behind. Moscow, Irina, the statue of Pushkin, the ring roads and the metro's circle line, Stalin's thoroughfares, the Western-style, multi-lane Novy Arbat, the Yaroslavl Highway and the rows of dachas embellished with carved wooden flourishes, the slack, weary, overworked land, are left behind. An empty freight train a hundred metres long zooms by outside the window. This is still Moscow: a mass of nineteen-storey prefab buildings in the middle of a mud pit, faint, glimmering lights trembling in their icy windows, a construction site – half-finished highrises with gaping holes in their walls. Soon they, too, will be silhouettes in the distance. This is no longer Moscow: a house collapsed under the snow, a wild, swaying pine forest covered with frost, a clearing blanketed with snow, a gentle mist trapped under piles of snow, darkness, a lone log house in an expanse of white, an unkempt apple tree in the yard, a mixed forest stiff with snow, the plank fences of villas, a ramshackle wooden barn. An unknown Russia frozen in ice opens up ahead, the train speeds onward, shining stars etched against a tired sky, the train plunging into nature, into the oppressive darkness lit by a cloudy, starless sky. Everything is in motion: snow, water, air, trees, clouds, wind, cities, villages, people, thoughts. The train throbs across the snowy land.

The girl could hear the man's heavy, peaceful breathing. He was looking at his hands; they were large and strong. The light from switching lanterns flashed on the surface of the ground below. Sometimes the view was blocked by train carriages standing on the tracks, sometimes the dark of the Russian night spread outside the window, here and there a faintly lit house flashed by. The man looked up, gave the girl a long, piercing once-over, and said with relief, 'So it's just the two of us. The shining rails carrying us to God's refrigerator.'

A stocky, uniformed old carriage attendant appeared in the doorway of the compartment and handed each of them clean sheets and a towel. 'No spitting on the floor. The passageway is cleaned twice a day. Your passports, please.'

Having received their passports, she left with a sneer. The man nodded after her.

'That old bag Arisa has militia powers. She keeps the drunks and whores in line. It's best not to mess with her. She's the god of heat on the train. Keep that in mind.'

He took a folded knife with a black handle out of his pocket, removed the safety catch, and pressed a button. There was a ringing of metal as the steel blade clicked and sprang open. He put the knife carefully on the table and dug a large chunk of Rossiskaya cheese, an entire loaf of black bread, a bottle of kefir and a jar of smetana out of his bag. Last he brought out a bag of pickles dripping salt water and started to pop them into his mouth with one hand while he devoured the black bread he held in the other. When he'd finished eating, he reached into the bag and took out a wool sock with a glass bottle of warm tea inside it. He looked at the girl for a long time. His eyes showed distaste at first, then a greedy curiosity, and finally some degree of acceptance.

'I am Iron Steelavich,' he said. 'Metal man and general labourer to the princes of Moscow. Vadim Nikolayevich Ivanov is my name. You can call me Vadim. Would you like some tea? It has vitamins, so it's good for you to drink a cup or two. I was thinking for a moment that they'd given this old codger a stiff sentence, put me in the same cage with an Estonian. There's a difference between the Finlyandskaya respublika and the Sovietskaya Estonskaya respublika. Estonians are hook-nosed German Nazis, but Finns are basically made from the same flesh as we are. Finlandiya is a little potato way up north. You people are no trouble. All the world's northern people are one tribe, a northern pride holds us together. By the way, Miss, you're the first Finn I've ever seen. But I've heard a lot about you. You Finns have prohibition.'

He poured her a glass of black tea. She tasted it warily. He savoured a small sip of his own, then got up and made his bed. He undressed modestly, taking off his outermost clothes, his thick black trousers with their narrow leather belt, his light jacket sewn from coarse fabric, and his white shirt, and folded them neatly at the end of the bed. He pulled on striped, sky-blue pyjamas and crept in between the starched sheets. Soon his cracked heels and toes, twisted from poor shoes and neglect, emerged from under the blanket.

'Good night,' he said with a bland look on his face, almost whispering, and fell immediately asleep.

The girl was awake for a long time. The shadows of the tea glasses moved around the dim compartment without lighting on anything. She had wanted to get away from Moscow because she needed distance from her own life, but now she was already yearning to go back. She thought about Mitka, Mitka's mother Irina, Irina's father Zahar, and herself, how they were all doing. She thought about their temporarily shared home, which was empty now. Even the cats, Miss Dirt and Tom Trash, were gone. The engine whistled, the rails screeched, the rattling train pounded metallically, the man snored quietly all night long. The sound reminded her of her father and she felt safe. Finally, in the wee hours, as the shadows began to dwindle, she fell into a frothy, white dream.

WHEN SHE WARILY OPENED HER EYES, the first thing she saw was the man doing push-ups between the beds. A green glimmer of sunlight played over the lacquered walls of the compartment; the man wiped the sweat from his brow with a towel. Before she had time to sit up there was a knock at the door and Arisa, who had stuffed herself into her black uniform jacket, brought in two steaming glasses of tea, moist waffles, and four large cubes of Cuban sugar, and put them on the table. The man dug some kopecks out of his wallet, which was decorated with an embossed picture of Valentina Tereshkova in her space helmet.

When Arisa had left he grabbed his narrow-bladed knife from under the bed, picked up a sugar cube in his left hand, knocked the cube in two with the dull side of the blade, and handed the girl a steaming glass of tea and half a cube.

He gave a shy, melancholy smile, took out a bottle of vodka, opened it, and filled two blue shot glasses that he dug from the depths of his bag.

'Our shared journey may be a long one, but my speech will be short. A toast to our meeting. A toast to the world's only real power, the Soviet Union. The Soviet Union will never die!'

He tossed the shot down his throat and bit off a juicy piece of onion. The girl lifted her glass to her lips, but didn't drink.

He dried his lips on the edge of the tablecloth, smiling boyishly. The girl took a drink of tea. It was well-steeped, aromatic and strong. That's when he noticed that she hadn't drunk her vodka.

'It's sad to drink alone,' he said.

She didn't touch the glass. He stared at her with a look of disappointment on his face.

'It's hard to understand. But all right. I won't make you, even though I'd like to.'

He was lost in thought, watching her from under his eyebrows. She didn't like the expression on his face, so she took the small towel and her toothbrush and headed for the WC for her morning wash.

There was a queue reaching halfway down the corridor. The travellers were wearing their dressing gowns, pyjamas, tracksuits, a couple of men in nothing but white army longjohns.

More than an hour later she reached the front of the queue. It was her turn to grab the wet, sticky door handle. The WC was filthy and the stench was pungent. Pee and soap and wads of newspaper floated around on the floor. Not a drop of water came out of the tap. There were two paltry, sharp-cornered fragments of beige-brown soap broken from a larger bar, smelling of soda. One piece was covered in a rusty-brown slime. She stepped up onto the toilet so she wouldn't wet the slippers she'd bought in Leningrad, and managed to dry-clean her teeth and face. The little window of the WC was open a crack. An abandoned, forgotten station was passing by.

The man loaded the table with black bread, canned horseradish, chunks of onion and tomato, mayonnaise, canned fish, and boiled eggs which he carefully peeled and sliced in two.

'God doesn't forget the well-fed, and vice versa. So help yourself.'

They ate for a long time, and when he'd put the remains of the breakfast back in his bag of food and wiped the breadcrumbs off the table onto the floor they enjoyed their tea, which had cooled now.

'I had a dream about Petya last night. He and I were born the same year and we were in the same grade at school. Five and a half years together. School didn't suit us – we had to go to work. I met the trucks at the market steps and when they arrived I threw the goods from the trucks into the warehouse. Petya hauled boards at a construction site. We lived in a boiler room. There was one window, you could see the pavement, people's feet going by. That's where we were living. Then one evening Petya didn't come home from work. I took the trolley to the construction site the next day to ask about him and they said that he had been run over by a machine and killed. They said the machine had killed him. I asked what machine. One old guy pointed to a wretched little excavator. Said that it was the culprit. I took a sledgehammer and smashed it beyond repair. Since then I've been on my own.'

She glanced at him, deep in his thoughts, and thought about Mitka and an early morning in August. They'd been sitting on a concrete bench at the edge of Pushkin Square smoking pot, waiting for dawn, when a drunken gang of young people showed up and started to push and threaten them. They pushed past the group and hurried away, but one fat, bald-headed goon went after them and threatened to 'knock the four-eyes' brains out'. They were scared. They ran down the deserted street and a car appeared at the other end of the street and she was sure that it would have more skinheads in it. They went down a side street, cut across courtyards, and sprinted sweatily to their door.

'The first time I was in south Siberia was at the beginning

of the sixties. It was at the time of the monetary reforms. A rouble wasn't worth anything, you couldn't get food with good money, and they were asking fifty kopecks for a pint at the beer stand. I used to sit in the canteen on the site drinking some swill with Boris, Sasha and Muha the Dog. One day a work official came in, this felt-booted bumpkin, and said, Comrade, go to Sukhumi, in the Crimea, southern Siberia, they need crack workers out there. He shoved a piece of paper in my hand and disappeared like he was sucked under the floor. I went and told Vimma thanks for the pussy and see you later, my dear fat-assed bitch, and headed for the station and rode a rattly train across the wide open spaces of the Soviet Union. I ended up in Yalta instead of Sukhumi. They were building all kinds of little cabins, and when I told them I was a human machine, a Stakhanovite concrete hero, I got work immediately. It was the best summer of my life. I did nothing but lay around and whore. Girls who when you asked them if they were wet yet, they were, in about two minutes. Sometimes I went with one of them to the movies at the Construction Worker to see an adventure flick. *Three Men in the Snow. Lost in the Ice.* And what was that one I liked … *Three Friends on the High Sea.* Whenever I remember that summer my mouth waters. Life wasn't tied down with good sense back then. But then came this last bitch. Katinka. Warbling, in her sugary voice, Let me wash your shirt. That's when my life ended, nothing ahead of me but the dark, bumpy road of an alcoholic, sinking deeper all the time.'

An east wind sprinkled the white plain with lonely snowflakes, a pale glimmer flashed over the trees. He spat angrily over his left shoulder into a corner of the compartment.

'I'm talking about the same Katinka who saw me off at the station yesterday. Her face was my doing. I came home drunk and then it started. Same mess every time. She started in with the same old argument. She didn't know how to stop, so I slapped her once, then twice. If she'd just keep her mouth shut like a good girl, help a poor traveller take off his clothes, make a good supper. But she never learns. I try to explain, I even praise her. But she doesn't listen, she just lays it on thicker, screaming about how men built this damned world just for themselves. That's how a henpecked husband's anger can build up, and then I slap her till she's quiet. If she doesn't shut up then I knock her a good one right in the mouth. It's not easy for me – I don't like hitting – but it always happens that way. I have a right to speak too, to be a human being in my own home, even if I'm not there very often.'

He laid careful stress on each word, dropping them one by one. The girl tried to close her ears.

'It's depressing to have the same old fight in the middle of the night. It takes all the joy out of life. Last night there was a strong whiff of her rolling over me like a tank in my dreams. Just the thought of her wreck of a pussy makes me want to puke my guts out.'

The train gave a lurch, his hand jerked, and a tear rose in the corner of his eye. He wiped it away with the back of his hand and closed his eyes, cleared his throat and sat up straight, filled his lungs with air and blew it out again.

'But there's a limit to everything. I never hit Katinka out in the hall of the communal apartment, or in the street, or at the office. I only hit her in our own room, because otherwise the block watch or the militia would show up and I don't like either one of them, especially the militia. The number one rule is to not let the boy see it – after all, it is his mother. He's so big now that he has his own little woman to smack around. I don't like that ... Beat your wife with a hammer and you turn her into gold, that's what the old guys told me when I was a young man. It's advice I've followed. Maybe too much.'

The girl looked first at the floor, then at a frozen cloud at the edge of the sky. She'd never met a Russian man like this before. Or maybe she had, but she hadn't wanted to remember it. No Russian man had ever spoken to her like this. Still, there was something familiar about him, his insolence, his way of drawing out his words, his smile, his tender, disdainful gaze.

'Katinka is a Russian woman, ruthless and just. She works, takes care of the home and kids, she can handle anything. I just think differently than she does. Take my old mother, for instance. We all live next to each other in the same communal apartment, and I think it's a great thing – Katinka can cook for the old lady at the same time she cooks for herself and the boy, and keep a lookout, make sure Ma's life has some flavour to it. But it isn't that easy. For all the twenty-three years we've been married that bitch has been demanding that I throw my old mother out.'

The girl got up from the bed to go into the corridor, but he grabbed her tightly by the arm and pointed at the bunk.

'You're going to hear this to the end.'

She tore herself free. He dashed at her and seized her by the wrist, firm but fatherly. She slumped down on the foot of the bed.

He went back to his place, lifted a fingertip to his lips, and blew, smiling obscenely.

'Something that's always baffled me is how every suitor loves his bride, but every husband hates his wife. As soon as the marriage licence is signed the man turns into a clod and the woman turns into an old bag and discontent starts to gnaw away at both of them. The broad thinks that once they get some of the creature comforts then everything will be all right. She thinks the answer is her own hotplate, a new dressing gown, a floor vase, a kettle without any dents in it, a china tea set. The fellow, on the other hand, thinks, man, if I could get myself a whore, I could stand that old bag a little better. But in spite of everything ... Sometimes when I look real hard at Katinka, I feel like I want to say, Katyushka, my silly little thing, my little fool.'

He gave a heavy sigh, reached for the pickle bag, got hold of a pickle, popped it in his mouth, and accidentally swallowed it whole.

'Us men have nowhere to go. The dames would get by better without us. Nobody needs us, except another man. Right now I feel like drinking a toast to the energy, the toughness, the patience, the courage, the humour, the shrewdness, the deceitfulness and beauty of the Russian woman. It's the dames that keep this country going.'

He slid his hand under his bunk and pulled out a Tchaikovsky chocolate bar. He opened the wrapper with his knife and offered some to the girl. He didn't take a piece for himself, just put the bar down in the middle of the table. The chocolate was dark and tasted of naphtha. She thought of Irina, of how she would often sit under the reading lamp in her favourite armchair in the evening and read a book, how the yellow light from the lamp fell on the book's pages, how Irina's hands held the book, how her face ...

'Women used to know how to keep quiet. Nowadays they got their traps open all the time. One of the bitches used to put out and smoke at the same time, while I was fucking her. I wanted to strangle her.'

A birch forest, weary with hard frosts and sharp winds, came into view. The naked trees drew graphic lines in the snow. The train sped by, the snow blew into the air and hung there pure and sparkling. Sometimes the window was filled with frozen white forest, other times with blithe, blue, cloudless sky. The girl could hear the tones and rhythms of the man's voice. His momentary passion quickly evaporated, replaced by a hint of deep sadness.

He thought for a long time. His wet lips moved, now quickly, now very slowly. His posture had fallen; he was sitting with his shoulders drooped. The girl took her drawing things out of her bag and started to draw.

He glanced at her, sighed a little, shrugged his shoulders lamely.

'Katinka. My own Katinka.'

Silence fell over the compartment. He put his head against the cold windowpane. She got up and went out.

Several passengers were standing in the corridor. A freight train was going past in the other direction, causing their train to rock. The little station building flashed like a turquoise dot in a vast universe. A splash of dirt had been thrown against the corridor window during the night, and a pale light filtered through it. The birches grew sparse, the train quieted its speed, a rusted wreck of metal lay on the neighbouring track, and soon the train was shooting into Kirov station. A sign along the track said that Moscow was about a thousand kilometres away.

The door of the carriage was open. She stood in the doorway. A few small snowflakes drifted in the still, dry cold of the day. A decrepit local train twitched restlessly at the next platform as if it was in the grip of a seizure. People pushed their way out of its innards, desperately gulping the fresh air. The station bell rang once, then twice. She had a glimpse of the black plastic peak of the guard's cap before Arisa came to close the door.

'What are you standing there for? Do you want to get off in Kirov? They'd horsewhip you here. Get back into your compartment! You don't have a citizen's passport, or an address here. Stupid foreigners don't understand anything, sticking their noses where they're not wanted! They foist all the unlucky ones on me. Do you even know who Kirov was?'

The girl tottered slowly back down the corridor of the moving train and looked at the swaying town outside the window. A pack of stray dogs were fighting in front of a baroque administration building and a young man was hitting them with a broken broomstick. She went to the stewardess's compartment to buy some tea. Arisa sat on the bed, all-powerful, and looked at her pityingly. Georg Ots was singing in Russian on a small transistor radio.

'Everybody's lives should be equal,' Arisa said. 'Either equally good or equally bad.'

She handed the girl two glasses of tea and three packets of biscuits instead of two.

'People can handle anything, when they have no choice. Now get back to your own compartment!'

The man sat on his bed. He wore a plaid shirt open over his white longjohns. Under the wrinkles of the white shirt peeped a sweaty, muscular belly. He picked up a small orange from the table and started to tear roughly at the peel. When he'd eaten the fruit he dug a tattered newspaper from under his bunk and blurted from behind it in an irritated tone, 'People are restless when they're young. No patience at all. Always rushing somewhere. Everything goes at its own pace. Time is just time.'

He wrinkled his brow and sighed.

'Look at me. An old duffer, a melancholy soul filled with a dull calm. A heart that beats out of sheer habit, with no feeling in it any more. No more pranks in him, not even any pain. Just dreariness.'

The girl remembered her last night in Moscow, how she'd hurried from one place to another, dashed down the long stairway into the metro and taken the red line to Lenin Library, run across the tiled floor of the museum-like station, through the maze of corridors lined with bronze statues and up the steep escalators to the blue line, ridden it past Arbat, got off at the church-like station decorated with mosaics whose name she couldn't remember now, and realised as she stood under a concrete arch that she'd forgotten her bag, which contained her train tickets and vouchers, had turned back the way she came, jumped off one metro train and onto another, gone through the stations where she'd changed lines and, to her great amazement, found her bag at the Lenin Library stop – it was waiting for her in the middle of the metro inspector's window.

The train braked and came to a stop. A moment later the engine gave a jerk and the train was moving again. Another brake. Another stop. The engine dithered for a moment, whistled cheerfully, made up its mind, and moved. The wheels rang in momentary apology but soon the train was rattling ahead with purpose. The sun bounced up from beyond a field of snow, lit up the land and sky for a moment, then disappeared behind the boundless swampy landscape. The man examined the girl sharply.

'So your soul's full of nothing but dreams? Well, go ahead and dream. Ivan the Fool falls asleep on the stove bench and dreams about a stove that moves and a table that fills itself with food, but this life that men wiser than me call a mere holding cell is here and now. Death may come tomorrow and grab you by the balls.'

His narrow face shone with self-satisfaction. He had a beautiful mouth, narrow lips and a small scar on his chin like Trotsky.

'Death can't be any worse than life.' He closed his eyes and pressed his lips tightly together. Then he hummed. 'Don't you fear death my girl, not as long as you're alive. If you're alive, then death's not here yet, and once you're dead, it's already gone.'

He hiccuped a little, shook his shoulders, and sat up straighter. 'I'd rather die than be afraid. If there's anything you should be afraid of, it's the Mongolians. They don't even have names. They don't do anything but eat, screw, sleep, and die. They have no morals of any kind. The human soul doesn't mean a thing to them. But they do know how to destroy. Give a Mongolian a transistor radio and five minutes later he'll hand back a pile of screws and wires and an empty case. The Mongolians have treated us Russians terribly and crushed the moral backbones of the likes of us, and still we try to help them. Try to bring them up to the present. But they don't understand anything. They screw their children and laugh right in our faces … Am I getting through to you? Look, the Soviet Union is a powerful country, a great, old, very diverse people lives here. We've suffered through serfdom, the time of the tsars, and the revolution. We've built socialism and flown to the moon. What have you done? Nothing! What do you have that's better than us? Nothing!'

He smacked his palms on his knees and opened his mouth to say something, but was silent.

Next to the train, far above the wall of forest, an eagle glided by with a calf carcass in its claws. The compartment door fell open. The little lamps that glimmered yellowish along the edge of the floor buzzed; the corridor looked like an airport runway. The heating vent threw out a burning heat in the narrow space. The girl went into the corridor. There was a young couple there, with a wrinkled old woman the size of a child, and a little girl in pigtails. The girl had a brown Pioneer teddy bear under her arm and in her lap a clown doll in a tall hat that looked like a schizophrenic who'd been through a bad trip. A violet sun over a shy forest clearing slipped behind the snow-covered evergreens. In the dense depths of the forest slept little birds in nests among the rocks, sinewy, white-coated hares in their burrows, and snoring bears in their hidden caves.

Arisa was making her rounds of the compartments and Sonechka, the younger stewardess in her oversized uniform, followed after her. The girl tried to talk with Sonechka, but she was so shy that she turned her face away at once and disappeared after Arisa into the first compartment. It was an area restricted to the carriage staff where an angrily bubbling samovar as big as the wall steadily puffed and steamed day and night. The samovar held a bucket of boiling water.

The slackening sun revolved briefly on the horizon. The dusky forest rose up humming towards a frail, cloud-embroidered sky. The man appeared in the passageway, and the girl went into the compartment, felt the rumble of the rails, and fell asleep.

When she woke up, he was looking at her with a very offended expression on his face. She smiled at him, thinking about how logical the whole thing was. She had left Moscow because now was the right time to realise her and Mitka's shared dream of a train trip across Siberia, all the way to Mongolia. True, she was making the trip alone, but there was a reason for that.

The man had taken a worn deck of cards out of his bag and started to play solitaire.

'Georgians,' he said. 'They've got legs like giraffes and they know how to sell themselves to fellows like me so well that you forget you paid for it. History has beaten the Armenians down, made them all humble lesbians and nice guys who won't discipline their children. A Tatar only likes Tatars, a Chechen is a combination of an excellent baby machine and a drug dealer, the Dagestanis are small, thin, ugly, and smell of camphor, and the foolishly proud Ukrainians are always plotting nationalist conspiracies in their horrible accents. A Russian gets to where he's deaf to it. And then there's the Balts. Half-assed. They have no secrets. Too practical. Walking around with their mouths turned down, eyes straight ahead.'

He tapped his fingers on the tabletop. The girl coughed wearily, but he didn't take any notice of this indication of her thoughts.

'I've never screwed a Russian woman who was satisfied, not even for a minute. And this cock has pumped thousands of different colours of pussy.'

He stretched his thick hands out towards her. Long fingers grew from them, the fingernails flat and clean. They were horrible hands. His expression was at first nonchalant, then plainly hostile.

'But tell me, what's someone like you doing on this train? Selling some cunt?'

The girl flinched, let out a feeble squeak, grabbed her winter boot from under her bunk and threw it at him, then got up and went out into the corridor. The heel of the boot hit him right in the temple. Once outside, she calmed herself for a long time before going to Arisa to ask for a different compartment.

Arisa listened to her request with her head to one side.

'We'll see,' she said, in such an unhurried manner that the girl handed her a twenty-five-rouble note.

Arisa apparently didn't feel it was a sufficient sum.

'It's against the law to change compartments. But perhaps I could do something to arrange it. It will be difficult, though.'

The girl slipped another banknote of the same value into her hand – it was all she could part with.

Arisa glanced at the note disdainfully.

'Getting around a rule like that is a tough job, in fact it's dangerous for me personally. I could lose my job or even end up in jail because of you. But perhaps it could be arranged ...'

The girl didn't listen to the rest of what she had to say. She rushed back out into the corridor with a sob in her throat. She simply had to swallow her defeat and go back to the man, at least at night.

The train sped with a whine across the flat, blustery landscape, under a sky frothy with winter clouds. A vibrant forest beyond an open field tossed a flock of sparrows at the sky. She calmed herself by watching the black, starkly drawn shadow of the train against the bright snow.

She thought about Irina, how she might be sitting in the smoking room of the chemistry institute, behind the Achievements in the National Economy pavilion, smoking a cigarette and getting ready for her next lecture. She thought about Zahar, who could see through her, and Mitka, who was good. A little kitten appeared in the corridor and looked at her beseechingly. She picked it up and held it and petted its rumpled fur. At the insane asylum, Mitka had said that socialism kills the body and capitalism kills the spirit but socialism the way we have it harms both the body and the spirit.

When Mitka was turning eighteen, she and Irina had the task of finding food to cook for his birthday party. They had started gathering ingredients back in November, and had managed to find all kinds of things, but Irina wasn't satisfied. One morning they went out to hunt for groceries at six a.m. They rushed through the dry, freezing weather to the Yelisev shop, but they didn't find anything there, not even baked *bubliks*. Angry, they hopped onto a freezing tram, and rode past the Boulevard and the snowy maples to the fragrant bread shop in Bronnaya. There they found a small loaf of good bread. They got on the trolleybus, which was so hot that they were soon covered in sweat, and trundled hopefully to Zach-aczewski Lane. There was a grocery there where Irina had once found two cans of high-quality sardines. They didn't find any-thing, though, not even pickles. They stood for a moment in the windy street, uncertain what to do, where to go. They walked with frozen toes, arm in arm, to Lenin Street, but the trip didn't add any weight to their shopping bag. They jogged over to Timiryazev. There they found a bottle of cologne for Yuri, but nothing to eat. They swung by Chistiye Prudy on the bus, brought Yuri his cologne, and got six eggs from him. Why not go to the currency exchange shop? he asked. I don't have any dollars, the girl whispered, we already blew all of it, plus my salary, at the beginning of autumn. Yuri yelled after them to go to the market, for God's sake, although he knew that there was nothing there. On Sokolniki Street they found two big jars of borscht, put them under their arms and headed proudly to the tram stop on Tverskoy Boulevard, and Irina glanced at her watch and said that she should have been lecturing at the institute a long time ago. A country woman was shivering in front of the paper shop. The girl bought a handsome gladiolus from the woman and handed it to Irina, and just as they were about to leave, the woman whispered that she had two chickens in her bag. Were they interested? Of course! Irina said, and settled on a price. They ran to the nearest metro station. Irina took the blue line to the insti-tute and the girl went home on the yellow with her bag of chickens. Zahar was home and she asked him to come in the kitchen and opened her bag and there they were, two sweet, fluttering brown chickens with rubber bands wrapped around their beaks. Zahar looked at them and said that with a few weeks of seed feed they would be ready to stew. They took the squawking chickens into the bathroom. She laid some of the laundry on the bottom of the tub as a cushion. The wooden towel rack served as a perch. They called the little one Plita and the big one Kipyatok. The day before Mitka's party Zahar slaughtered the fattened chickens expertly in the bathroom and plucked them on the balcony. Then Irina taught her and Mitka how to cook chicken the Stalinist way.

A grey half moon sprinkled light over the snowy, silent, melancholy forest, keeping gleaming red Mars company. A little boy was singing to himself while he played with a whistle shaped like a rooster at the other end of the carriage's corridor. When the nocturnal light of the moon dimmed and turned dirty, the girl returned to her compartment. She was hungry and tired.

The compartment smelled like Consul hair tonic, the kind you can buy at Party hotel kiosks. The man looked at her from the end of the trail of scent, shyly, it seemed.

'Feeling better?'

A draughts board had appeared on the table, a little battery-less Blaupunkt travel radio with a little green cat's-eye light, and a travel samovar, cheerfully bouncing and puffing steam. He had put loose tea in the enamel kettle and was pouring boiling water over it.

'Sorry about that cunt comment. Devil got into me. Dark forces.' He felt his temple proudly. There was a little mark there. Then he pointed at her boot, which he had placed in the middle of the floor. 'You did the right thing. I deserved to have my arse kicked.'

She smiled.

'Thank you, my girl. There are two kinds of anguish in life: when we want to and can't, and when we can but we don't want to.'

She got out her food, put it on the table, and started to eat. She offered some to him too, but he wasn't hungry.

When she'd finished eating, she took Garshin's *The Scarlet Flower* out from under her bottle of whisky and started to read. Mitka had given it to her and said that it showed how a sick mind worked. She was slowly reading the dog-eared, brown-paged book, printed in the previous century.

'The attendants undressed him in spite of his desperate resistance. His disease had doubled his muscular strength, and he easily tore himself from the hands of several keepers, dashing them to the ground; at last, four of them got him down, and, taking him by the hands and feet, put him into the warm water. It seemed to him boiling, and through the frenzied brain flashed a fragmentary, incoherent thought of torture by scalding water and red-hot iron. Choking, and convulsively beating the water with hands and feet (as far as the firm hold of the keepers allowed), he shrieked out in strangled tones an incoherent speech, such as no one could imagine without hearing it.'

She put the book on the table. Oh, Mitka!

The man gently packed away his radio and threw himself on his bunk. The late, narrow moon hovered slack above the wild landscape.

'The ice seems to be broken, my girl,' he said lightly. 'Now I can go to sleep. Life is easier when you're asleep.'

She watched him as he puffed in his sleep. There was something about him. Maybe it was his cauliflower ears. His way of holding his knife. His flat, muscular stomach. She felt the glow in the west colour the universe purple for a moment and the stars ignite in the black sky one by one.

She thought about Mitka, his long eyelashes, his perfect toes, his inward smile. The day they ran through the freezing rain to the Armaments Museum and hid inside a tank and the museum guard found them after the place had closed. They ended up sitting up all night with him in the guard's booth clinking champagne glasses. Mitka, whose door always had to be open, had gone to the mental hospital to avoid the army, deployment to Afghanistan.

The night had already chilled through the dark into a red dawn coming in through the window. The yellow moon swept up the last bright star to make way for the fiery sun, and slowly all of Siberia grew light. The man was in his blue tracksuit bottoms and white shirt, doing push-ups between the beds, his forehead sweaty, his eyes sleepy, his mouth dry and stinking, a thick stench in the room, an airless window, silent tea glasses on the table, quiet crumbs on the floor. A new day was before them, with its orange, frost-covered birches and pine groves where hidden animals roamed and fresh snow drifted over the plains, white, fluttering longjohn legs, limp penises, mitts and muffs and cuffs and flowered flannel nightgowns, shawls and wool socks and straggly toothbrushes.

THE NIGHT SPEEDS THROUGH THE DARK into dim morning, a dogged queue at the shrine of the WC, a dry wash among the puddles of pee, sputum, shame, sheepish looks, shadows of steaming tea glasses in the windows, large, flat cubes of Cuban sugar, paper-light aluminium spoons, black bread, Viola cheese, sliced tomatoes and onion, the roasted torso of a young chicken, canned horseradish, hard-boiled eggs, salt pickles, mayonnaise, tinned fish, and canned peas from Moldavia.

The darkness breaks out in a new day, snow rising from the ground up the tree trunks, the silence fading in their upper branches, a hawk perched on a turquoise cloud, looking down at the slithering worm of train.

Quiet spread orange over the snowy taiga. The man sat on the edge of his bunk, placed teacups on the table, and waited impatiently for the girl to look at him.

'Once, in Moscow, there was a father, a mother, and a son. On 65 Kropotkin Street, in a little room behind a communal kitchen, in a home where locks couldn't protect them. This family was quite ordinary, the mother working behind the counter in a bread shop, the father drinking on a construction site, but a true Stakhanovite nonetheless. Late one evening, when he thought the boy was asleep, the man said to his wife, It's the boy or me. The wife whispered back in a sweet voice, Wait another month and he'll be gone.'

He wiped his nose with his palm and swallowed.

'In the morning the boy said his goodbyes to his one-eyed

dog and pulled the door shut behind him. By nightfall he had joined a gang of other runaways and started living on the streets of Moscow. These street children slept wherever and whenever they could, in a heap like puppies, together with the deformed and the crippled, the thieves, whores, mental patients and hunchbacks. Nobody missed them, but they, too, wanted to live. The less bread they had, the more misery they had, the greater their desire to live became. They knew no fear because they were so young that they didn't yet know the value of life. They didn't know themselves and they didn't know the world. This boy grew up on the streets. He grew up to be a shaggy, iron-belted Soviet Citizen who pissed pure vodka.'

He poured steeped tea into both glasses and added hot water from the samovar to get it to the right strength.

'Tell me, do you know why a rainbow never forms behind the back of the person looking at it?'

There was a thud, a knock, and then the train braked furiously. The rails trembled, the carriages swayed, the snow on the roadbed flew into the air. The train jerked along with the brakes screeching for some distance. Boxes toppled off the shelves and the tea glasses smashed against the wall of the compartment. A woman screamed, children cried, someone ran down the corridor with heavy steps.

Arisa's calming voice could be heard. 'Don't worry. Everything's normal. Citizens, please stay in your compartments. There's nothing to see here.'

The man opened the door a crack. The passageway was filled with the curious. The girl looked out of the window and saw only forest smothered in snow. The man went into the corridor and she followed him. The door to the next carriage was open, the people crowding off the train, some bareheaded, some wearing slippers. The man shoved his way through the people and jumped into the snow among the staring, clamorous crowd. The girl remained standing in the crush on the top step of the carriage doorway. She could see drops of blood dripping into the pure white of the snow a short distance ahead. Her gaze followed a tree trunk up towards the sky. Among the pine branches hung an elk's bloody leg.

'The animal's suffering. We have to finish it,' Arisa sputtered. 'Bring the axe, quick!'

The axe swung in Arisa's hand as she waded towards the engine. The three-legged elk was breathing quickly, terror glittering in its eyes. Arisa lifted the axe and struck its sharp blade into the middle of the elk's head. The blade sank into its skull, but it didn't die.

Shaking his head, the man strode over to the twisting, bellowing animal, grabbed his jackknife from the side of his boot, snapped the blade open, and stuck it into the elk's jugular vein. Blood sprayed in an arc and landed in the snow, then it was very silent for a moment.

'The journey continues!' Arisa shouted sharply, shooing the passengers back onto the train.

On the train, the man wiped his knife on his bootleg, folded it closed, slid his hand up his side, looking for his trouser pocket, and slowly, with a slight smile, slipped the knife in. The girl waited for the train to roll into motion.

'Once we were on a trip to Pskov to renovate a convent. We were sitting in third class, drinking. The train was rattling quietly onward across snowy nature, just like now. In the middle of this game I felt the carriage shudder. Then it started to lean and the old ladies started screaming. I looked out of the window and saw shards of railway sleepers fly by and the snow on the ground getting closer and closer. One sharp turn and the ground under the train embankment filled the window, and then the carriage was on its side in the snow. I thought I'd died and everybody else had too. But it was nothing, just a few bloodied heads, crawling out from any exit we could find. Some genius who needed the iron had stolen a stretch of the rails. We walked along the tracks for three days before we saw the towers of Pskov Kremlin. We got there, put on a couple of new roofs, and in the spring when the rails had been replaced and the guilty party found and executed, we took the same train back to Moscow.'

The girl dug her headphones out of her bag, flopped onto her bunk, closed her eyes, and listened to music. She fell asleep, switched from Louis Armstrong to Dusty Springfield, and fell asleep again.

THE TRAIN HAD SPED through the Udmurt Republic, and now was dragging limply past the Balezino station. The man rubbed his chin. The girl was listening to the choked puff of the small air vent and drawing. The morning stared sternly at them. The man opened up a draughts board and set out the pieces. The girl chose black.

They played three games, of which she won two. He congratulated her with a fierce squeeze of her hand.

The white sun rose high and hearty above the snowy woodland. Smoky clouds rushed to the centre of the sky looking for a resting place. The man and the girl sat silently. They sat in their own thoughts for a day or two.

It had been a sunny turquoise summer day. When Irina's girlfriend Julia left, the girl went into Irina's bedroom and looked down at Bakunin Street. People were walking in their spring coats. The girl even saw a couple of stylishly cut, flowered summer dresses. Just as she was about to look away, she noticed three men under the old maple trees. Something strange was going on among them – quick movements, lurches, swinging motions, sudden slumps. Then she saw a red blood stain on one thin man's white shirt. One of the other men ran away. She saw him throw a knife down in a driveway. One stabbed man fell to the ground, another rolled on the pavement holding his stomach. There was a truck in front of the bakery. Five workers were lounging on the back of the truck. They ran after the stabber, got hold of him, and knocked him down. All five of them started to hit and kick him. Soon there were dozens of people around him, mostly women, beating him with handbags and gigantic sweet potatoes. The girl's gaze shifted to the stabbed men. They were both lying motionless. No one was interested in them. A militia car arrived and the crowd around the stabber reluctantly dispersed. Blood poured out of the beaten man's mouth and ears; his head had swollen to the size of a watermelon; one of his legs was bent in an unnatural position. There were two militiamen. They dragged the horrifying pile of flesh over to their Lada and then straightened their backs as if they were pondering how to cram the dying killer into the little car. When one of them grabbed him to shove him into the back seat, he wrenched himself free and hopped on one foot, vomiting blood, and got into the car.

After a grating screech of the train's brakes, the Perm station slid across the window. The girl glanced at the man who was bleating in his sleep, moaning, trembling, muttering to himself.

She heard Arisa's voice in the corridor. 'There's nothing in this town but drunken soldiers.'

The girl watched the wind wrestle with the disintegrating carcass of a cardboard box wandering the empty rails. A flat-looking dog the size of a calf lapped brown water from a hole in the ice that covered a puddle of sludge. Soon the engine whistled shrilly and the train picked up speed. Perm, the last city before the Urals, was left behind. Rimsky-Korsakov's bitterly jaunty song 'Pesnya Varyazhskogo Gostya' chirped from the loudspeakers. The view from the window was sometimes obscured by passing trains, sometimes fences, warehouses, large buildings, buildings under construction or demolition, light, darkness, barracks, fences, power lines, an endless criss-cross of wires, scrap metal, ravaged landscape, light, darkness, wild nature, an old train engine passing. Perm was left behind. The man slept peacefully in his bed, a soft expression on his face. The girl read Garshin's *The Scarlet Flower:*

'He left the door-step. Glancing round, but not seeing the keeper, who was behind him, he stepped across the bed and stretched out his hand to the blossom, but could not make up his mind to pick it. He felt a burning and pricking sensation, first in the outstretched hand, then through all his body, as though some strong current of a force unknown to him flowed from the red petals and penetrated through his whole frame. He drew nearer and touched the blossom with his hand, but he fancied that it defended itself by throwing out a poisonous, deadly vapour.'

She didn't feel anxious any more. She thought about Mitka's description of the mental hospital – a place where even the crazy are in danger of going crazy. She liked the book's sick main character so much she would have liked to read more about him, his strange, twisted world. Mitka's world. She thought about the mental hospital in the book and the hospital where Mitka was. Had anything changed in a hundred years? Perhaps there was a little less water on the floor of Mitka's room than there was in the patient's room in the book. How long would it take for things to change here? Could time really change anything?

The Ural mountains glimmered far off, low and insignificant. They weren't impressive. The range remained slightly ahead, then a sign flashed by at a stop with an arrow pointing west that said 'Europe' and one pointing east that said 'Asia'.

A few hours later the mountains started very slowly to recede behind them.

The girl slept, and awoke when the man waved something under her nose. His knife? She opened her eyes, alarmed.

'You'll grow too much, little one, if you sleep so long. Your arse will get fat. Watch out.'

He looked at her with playful sternness for a moment and put the paper carnation back in the vase.

Burning clouds dashed across the southern sky, headed north. A lukewarm sun fought its way through the tops of the tallest spruce trees. Old birches decorated in a fluff of frost like blooming bird cherries graced a derelict garden. She sat up in bed with her eyes closed. Concentrated. Lifted both hands to the top of her chest near her throat and tried to calm her breathing.

After a moment she opened her eyes and looked for her headphones. She looked at the man. He opened his mouth without looking at her.

'It often happens that I think I'm going to do one thing and I do another. As a young man, when I was screwing Vimma, I thought I'd never give up that pussy. But then what happened? I played cards with the boys and lost everything, even my coat and my leather belt. When there was nothing else left, I bet Vimma. I lost. And Vimma disappeared like a bunny in a magician's hat, and I never saw her again.'

He poured water into the samovar and turned it on, measured a small spoonful of tea into the enamel pot. Then they just waited for the water to boil, the tea to steep, to pour it into the glasses.

'If we were lice, or maybe bedbugs, I'd be the kind of

bedbug that hunkers down and doesn't move and stares at something that nobody else can see. You, on the other hand, would dash around until you died from exhaustion. But if we were cockroaches, we'd hook up with our own crowd straight off. They take good care of each other, help each other out at every turn. We'd take responsibility for everything that happened between us. What is a crowd? It's a partnership, a gang. It always sticks together. The cockroaches are right. For good or ill.'

The train braked softly as it approached Sverdlovsky. Lights and shadows slid peacefully past. The soft, frozen winter dusk beckoned along the side streets of the town, its parks and squares. A local train squeaked on the next track. A wave of people arriving from the suburbs flooded into the small station from an arriving train, a full moon reflected orange from drifts of snow yellowed with dogs' piss. The stars in the sky were like a vast array of portals to another reality, the same stars as in Moscow, but different.

The train rocked and accelerated. It was soon speeding forward, and all the villages that had sprung up east of the city long ago were left far behind. The man tossed and turned in his bed with his clothes on. The girl put her headphones over her ears and closed her eyes. The music carried her to autumn in Moscow, the grey-bearded doorman raking dry autumn leaves, the light from the university hallway, the fresh-painted smell of the handrail, the simple beauty of the office coat rack.

As a perfect, velvet-black night opened up outside the window, the man finally undressed bashfully, slid between the covers, and turned his back to her, not even wishing her goodnight. She was tired, but couldn't sleep. She lay awake, staring at Russia's deep darkness until finally, when night was nearly morning, she pulled her head into a hood of blanket and fell into restless dreams.

In the morning she stopped in to see the carriage staff. Arisa was cleaning the entrance and Sonechka was sitting alone in the compartment with her back towards the door. The girl ordered two teas and some *bubliks*. Sonechka nodded, but didn't turn to look at her. As she was leaving, Arisa backed out of the entrance carrying a bucket made of Latvian tin.

'Kirov was a great leader in Leningrad who was stabbed in the back by Stalin. First they slaughter their enemies together with their allies, then the allies together with their friends, then their friends. They draw lots for the rest. No one is innocent. A person is always dissatisfied with something, and it's always discovered. The guilty party is always found, and his offence, too, within a day of his arrest. Remember that.'

The girl returned to her compartment, lay down, and pretended to sleep. She thought of the three years she'd studied in Moscow. Her first year had been spent in a tight-knit crowd of Finnish students that had dispersed when Maria went back to Finland and Anna went to Kiev. Then she made friends with Franz. Franz was a West Berlin philosophy student who idolised Ulrike Meinhoff and had a habit of pursing his lips contemptuously when he disagreed about something. One day Franz quit his studies and returned to West Berlin. So she was left alone and took the opportunity to get to know Mitka.

A few *versts* later the man awakened with a jolt and sat up without opening his eyes. His greasy hair was pasted to his head.

There was a sharp, crisp knock on the door. 'Here's your tea, comrades,' Arisa said in a dry, cross voice.

The girl quickly grabbed some coins from her small coin purse and paid her. The man looked at her in wonder.

'I'll take care of the tea. Is that clear?'

The girl nodded, abashed. Snowy hillocks like clouds grew beyond the drab evergreens on their side of the train. The last hills of the Urals.

'Don't fret, my girl. Everyone wants to feel needed. I understand, but there are certain rules in life that every citizen has to follow. You're here as my guest.'

He groped under his pillow for a cigarette and lit it. He opened the compartment door and stood leaning in the doorway.

'Life just vanished in a strange red mist. There's nothing left of it. Or maybe a little piece of it. Maybe a little piece of life at the bottom of your pocket.'

He smoked his cigarette with one eye closed.

'Whenever I go home to Moscow after being away for a long time, everything looks sad. And when I leave with my suitcase full of darned socks and pressed underwear, I think that I'll never come back again, that this is the last time. I always go back. When I'm home I'm as bored as a prisoner on death row, but I tell Katinka that everything's fine. A person can't live without deceiving himself.'

Arisa dashed out of her compartment with a broomstick in her hand.

'Smoking here? Three-rouble fine! Right here in my hand, you old goat.'

He handed her a bill indifferently.

'Think you can buy yourself privileges, you fool? It's not that easy. I ought to drown you in the latrine. You disgust me.'

He brushed his hair away with his hand and slapped Arisa on the backside. Arisa disappeared without looking back. He sat down on his bunk.

'Katinka can sure salt a cucumber. I've knocked her up sixteen times and she's had fifteen abortions.'

The girl gave him a dark look and let her tea glass fall over onto the table. The hot tea splashed on his bare toes. He grunted, flashed her a questioning look, and started whistling a lively soldiers' march with a satisfied sound, curling his red toes to the rhythm.

'Do you know, my girl, what the difference is between screwing and mating? Screwing is a fun, cheerful activity, while mating is a heavy, joyless task. So how about some screwing?'

He licked his lower lip. The girl's breathing was full of long pauses.

'Katinka's turned mouldy; that's why our life in Moscow is nothing but a dry fuck.'

He scratched the back of his neck with his left hand, then with his right, then put both hands on his chin and looked at her with mawkish helplessness. The grim mood in the compartment made for a tight squeeze. The girl looked at his hands. They were tough and demanding.

'If you don't want anything else, what about in the mouth? I'm just so damned tired of hiding in the corner and jerking off.'

The girl wiped her lips dry with the back of her hand.

'Or if that's no good, just one in the cheek would be all right. Strictly no hands. Georgian style.'

He unfastened his belt. 'You're not exactly a honey-pot, but you'll do. Same kind of bitch as all the rest. But that's all right. Twat comes with, arse is extra!'

Her eyes burned with unshed tears, which she tried to get rid of with a cough. He looked at her now and a worried expression came over his face.

'Are you catching a cold? I'll make you some medicine. Get some vodka, add some pepper and a dash of honey. That'll kill a flu.'

He started looking for his vodka bottle. The girl yanked open the compartment door and left.

A frozen marsh of delicate, snowy grasses bloomed in the train window. The landscape continued hour after hour almost the same, but constantly changing with the light. A blue thicket and a snowbank flashed across the frozen plain. A wavering line of men in grey-blue quilted jackets and trousers walked along the ridge of a snowbank with pickaxes in their hands.

Dark, smoking clouds appeared in the sky, soon covering the shimmer of the sun completely, and an oppressive dimness fell over the icy landscape. The train braked and slowed. A three-legged dog hobbled along the flat gravel roadbed trailing a thin trickle of blood. The train arrived in Tyumen station.

'The train will stop for an hour or two,' Arisa shouted. 'In other words, as long as it likes.'

There was a heap of wooden boxes on the platform. The girl piled three of them together to climb up to the corridor window, took a cloth handkerchief out of her pocket, and wiped one of the panes clean.

When she'd cleaned the window she walked towards a

station building veiled in dark red billowing mist. She went around the building and stopped at the south end. The station was ugly and dilapidated, the gutters were broken and pieces of the tin roof hung over the upper windows. The foundation was cracked in several places. The whole building slumped. Behind it she could see the glimmer of a dirty factory complex.

One of the tall oak doors was open and she followed a crippled crow into the station hall. The room was empty and spacious, the air damply cold and heavy, a skiff of fog floating above the quiet. Two white-toothed dogs dozed by the drinks stand; the smell of muffled talk and stale buns drifted from the coffee stall. A wandering photographer stopped her, showed her his Moskova 2 camera, and asked if she wanted a picture of herself. She didn't.

She stopped for a moment at the entrance to the buffet before going to the counter to order pickles and smetana. Twelve well-fed flies with glistening wings buzzed over the stained menus. Paper napkins blew from one table to the next. A leathery piece of meat, a watery gruel of macaroni casserole, and a cake decorated with pink icing roses stared at her from the glass case.

The station bell rang for the third time and the train rocked into motion. The oil town rose smouldering in the bright, frosty sunshine and hovered, all highrise rooftops gliding ever higher towards the lid of sky. The train sped past the freezing Soviet villages and housing areas. The limbo of unnamed towns was left behind. Pop music drifted from a distant compartment.

The marshy plain was left behind and a birch forest weighed

down with snow filled the land. The train moved in jerks now. A long line of freight trains carrying oil and coal appeared in front of the engine.

Hours, minutes, seconds later the train picked up speed and the oil towns and surrounding oil wells and towers with their black flames receded into the distance. In spite of many signs of spring, it was still winter in Siberia. Here and there on sheltered south slopes melted by the sun jutted last year's grasses. The innocent smell of wood smoke drifted into the carriage. The train slowed its speed and was soon moving at a crawl. As it passed an abandoned warehouse the trail of smoke thickened. Small fires danced in the grass right next to the rail track, beyond them the flames reached greedily towards the turquoise Siberian sky. Next to the train, in the middle of the cloud of smoke, an old woman ran around in a panic, her head bare, without a coat. Not just the grass but also the railway sleepers were burning, and the ruins of an old building as well. The wind whipped a cloud of red sparks against the iron bulk of the train. The flames flared for a moment, handsome and strong, but the Siberian frost dampened them. A young mother crumpled by life lifted her child in her arms and pointed at the smoking building receding behind them.

'Look, that's how granny's house burned down.'

The train skulked along for a considerable time before speeding up again. As darkness fell, the man came out of the compartment and stood next to the girl. Together they looked at the Irtysh River. The snow on the shores had shrunk; bare, snowless patches appeared among the drifts. At a narrow point in the current, in the middle of the channel, stood several immense concrete pillars. There had once been a bridge there, or else a bridge was being built and was abandoned. Far off on the horizon a power-plant town glimmered.

The man looked at the girl with a wary smile. 'I'm sorry, my girl. The devil got into me again. Lucifer himself. I just have such an urge to fuck. Go back in so you don't catch cold. Let me know when I can come in. I still have hope. When Ivan the Terrible turned eighty, he took a sixteen-year-old wife.'

The girl smiled in token of a sort of dry understanding and went into the compartment. She took a bottle of nail polish remover out of her bag, emptied it into his vodka glass, and slumped onto her bunk. She liked the man's Gagarin smile. She fell asleep to that, hungry, with all her clothes on.

The man gazed wistfully at the muddy river, sawmills along its shores, open, empty land around it as far as the eye could see. Under the cover of the ice the river rushed and swirled, a roiling current. In the wee hours the girl awoke and kicked the compartment door so that it hung half open. The man stepped immediately inside, gulped the contents of his vodka glass, and went to sleep without saying a word.

A RUDDY LIGHT PRESSED BRAZENLY in through the compartment window and divided the space. The man's bunk was left in shadow, the girl's in light. The man was fiddling with his nose. There was no sign whatsoever of the effect of the nail polish remover. Two tussell-feathered sparrows pecked at the corridor window.

'Arisa was here screaming about the engine needing a rest. So they're giving it a rest. What do you think, my girl, shall we go out? Take a look at the vodka shops of Omsk?' the man asked with solid self-certainty. 'Not on an empty stomach, though. First munch on a little something and then hit the streets. Hurrying can kill you. Remember that.'

The icy fog on the platform seized their breath so that they had to stand still for quite some time. Two hungry, nimble-footed dogs were barking on the platform. The station yard was filled with the bustle of work and the noise of travellers, screeching train engines, rattling luggage carts, clanging rails, curses, roars, and old women's uninhibited laughter. Among the stew of people a granny waving enormous mittens sold thick apple juice in large green bottles. The war in Afghanistan was accelerating and instead of food supplies the Soviet government was concentrating on arms production, and the girl hadn't been able to find anything but condensed milk, tinned fish, and random jars of mayonnaise in the Moscow groceries. There were nothing but problems everywhere. The toothpaste problem, the soap, sausage, butter, meat, and ever-present paper problem, even a doll problem. When she took a trip to Riga for the New Year, she found tomato juice and a three-litre jar of jam in an out-of-the-way food shop and nearly killed herself hauling them back to Moscow. She and Mitka enjoyed them until March. They had exchanged them for ballet and concert tickets, champagne, all kinds of things.

They got into a bus that was waiting in front of the station with a little parrot squawking on the dashboard. The bus sighed, bellowed, and puttered towards the town at walking pace. The man dozed off, the girl scratched a little hole in the frost on the window with her fingernails to let the light in. She watched a startled flock of cranes fly grandly along the shore of the Irtysh and disappear among the tall, green-balconied highrises. The factory chimneys looked like minarets.

The bus sagged and swayed and nearly toppled over as it dodged a group of oil workers crossing the road. Farther off beyond the city spread an endless stretch of ancient snow-covered pine forest.

The bus stopped with a yelp in front of the remains of Tara gate, the man woke up, and they hurriedly got out. Next to the gate was a low brick building with *Univermag* written on its side. A loudspeaker hung from a rusty, bent nail on one end of the shop. It dangled sadly in the winter wind, shreds of the pastorale from Tchaikovsky's *Queen of Spades* wafting around it.

In front of the shop entrance was a plain pine coffin lined with red silk. The edges of the coffin were decorated with black lace and on top of the lid was a bouquet of white and lemon-yellow carnations. Under the shop window was a snow-covered bench and on it lay a passed-out man with an accordion under his arm. They stopped at the coffin. The man took his hat off and made the sign of the cross. The shop door opened and a skinny old woman and four men with black crepe ribbons on the sleeves of their faded coats came out. The men picked up the white cloth sling, lifted the coffin off the ground and started walking towards the town centre. The funeral procession swayed down the slippery street, which was lined with a closely spaced row of electricity poles that looked like Orthodox crosses.

'May his troubled heart rest in peace,' the man said.

He wiped his brow as the procession disappeared behind a delicate mosque decorated with blue mosaics.

'When I was a young man I got sent to work on the peat bogs. There was one hard-fisted, low-browed fellow named Mishka. We made friends, if that's the right word for it. I never said a word to him, but we petted the same cat every evening ... Then it happened that one spring night in the wee hours, Mishka died. Somebody put two iron nails through his head. I asked the boss if I could go with him on his final journey. Can't do it, the boss said, the rules don't allow it. I stood there and watched while they carried Mishka up the hill. The backside of the pure white horse was decorated with dried bits of shit as it pulled the old manure cart behind it. In the cart was a box made of planks, and in the box lay Mishka.'

The man and the girl stood there quietly for another moment before they walked into the grocery shop. Torn flowered oilcloth covered the little counter. On it were arranged tins of tea, tubes of lotion, vermicelli, cheap perfume, and belt buckles. There were bars across the low window. A red-handed cleaning lady slopped a wet, ragged mop.

'Out. Can't you good-for-nothing arses see that we're cleaning here? Get out!'

Just as they were turning to leave, the shop assistant appeared from the back room, her enormous nose badly frozen.

'I can hear you!'

The man cleared his throat. 'No trouble here. Everything's peaceful.'

The shop assistant glanced at the cleaner and waved her hand.

'Varvara Aleksandrovna Pelevina, you may leave. The floor is fine.'

'My Ninka, may I have a couple of bottles of pepper vodka and a bunch of onions?' the man said.

'I'm not your Ninka!'

'Pepper vodka, my butter roll?'

'There isn't any.'

'But perhaps you have some … pepper vodka?'

'There isn't any.'

'How about a couple of mushroom pies and a bottle of mineral water?'

The shop assistant stared at him, surprised. Then she leered, swung her substantial rear end, and lifted a large bottle of clear liquor, a small bottle of Bear's Blood wine, a back-up bottle of Bulgarian swill, and a bunch of onions from behind the counter.

The man laughed, took out a few notes and a pile of kopecks, tossed them quickly into the little plate, picked up the bottles and the onions, gave the shop assistant a long look, flicked his tongue over his dry lower lip, and walked out of the shop with a bouncy step, and even a whistle. The girl remained in the shop for a moment, but soon left when the shop assistant gave her an angry look.

They walked to the bus stop. The wind increased and the rough sky spat out stinging, bitter snow that gathered its strength from somewhere far away on the tundra and froze the swaying spruce branches.

A bus stinking of rot eventually came, and they quickly got on. The driver was a bloated middle-aged woman, crammed into a fur-lined overcoat, who smelled strongly of onion liquor. The cold had spread through the bus and frozen over the windows. Layers of clouds rushed across the dark sky and sliced through each other, now just above the edge of the forest, now far up in the highest part of the sky.

They got off the bus at the station square. The wind blew a tattered black burlap sack around the statue of Lenin. They trudged tiredly to a ramshackle ice cream stand in a corner of the station with a sign on the door that read *Under refurbishment.*

The bar smelled of Lysol. Puddles of milk lolled over the beautifully tiled floor; the leaking milk cartons lay in the corner. The station was crammed with people. The man drank a glass of vodka, wolfed down a pie, and said he was going to get on the train.

The girl ordered a mayonnaise salad and a dish of ice cream topped with chocolate-covered plums and two kinds of biscuits.

The mayonnaise salad was just mayonnaise, the biscuits stuck out of the ice cream like stalks of hay. She looked at the asters on the windowsill, sad autumn flowers sitting tired in a vase without water. The lower sky covered itself in dark lumps of cloud, the higher part in sea-blue fluff. A tram swished heavily past.

She ate her ice cream unhurriedly. The biscuits she left on the edge of the plate.

The man rubbed his knees as she stepped into the compartment. A Tchaikovsky romance played from the beige plastic speakers.

Omsk is left behind. A closed city. Weary old, good old Omsk, sucked dry by the taiga, abandoned by youth. The prison where the young outlaw Dostoyevsky lay dying is left behind. The lifeless copy of a statue of Dostoyevsky in manhood is left behind. The city of Kolchak's White Guards is left behind. This is still Omsk: the lines outside the shoe shop, the tired land, the row of timber dachas faded grey. A lonely nineteen-storey building in the middle of a field, a five-hundred-kilometre oil pipeline, the yellow flames and black smoke from the oil rigs. Forest, groves of larch and birch, forest – these are no longer Omsk. A house collapsed under the snow. The train throbs across the snowy, empty land. Everything is in motion – snow, water, air, trees, clouds, wind, cities, villages, people, thoughts.

THE GIRL LISTENED TO MUSIC on her headphones and was on Bolshaya Sadovaya Street again. There, on the top floor of a green block of flats, was her and Mitka's secret place. Someone had painted a black cat on the wall of the ground-floor entrance and the stairwells were completely covered in quotes from Bulgakov's *The Master and Margarita*. How many times had she and Mitka walked up those narrow wooden stairs in the dark of night? Two steps were broken on the sixth floor, and if you didn't know about it you could fall straight to your death. But they knew about it, and they knew to be careful. On the highest landing, amid the stench of cat piss, was where she and Mitka had smoked their first joint together.

Her travelling companion bashfully changed his under-wear. He wrapped the dirty items in an old copy of *Literatur-naya Gazeta* and put the bundle in his suitcase.

The passengers who had boarded at Omsk were standing in the corridor. Among them was a Red Army officer and his old, translucently thin housekeeper. His uniform coat fitted him well and his shoes shone, as did his bloated face. He stood in the passageway with his back straight, periodically clearing his throat in a dignified manner. The man stared at him from the door of the compartment.

'The Soviet Union didn't have any officers in Lenin's day, just soldiers and commanders. You could only tell the differ-ence between them up close, by the emblems on their collars. Those days are long behind us. Nowadays the lieutenants and captains sit together at one table and the majors and colonels at another. That grimacing mug has a thief's look about him. He's probably a pansy, eating away at the spine of the Soviet Union.'

The officer's ears turned red and he took several stiff strides to stand in front of the man, then grabbed him by the nose and squeezed so hard that the man slumped back to his bunk and sat down.

'Hooligans will be thrown off the train at the next station,' the officer roared. 'If you were a little younger, I'd send you to the devil's kitchen for some re-education.'

The man was taken off guard, surprised by the officer's swiftness. 'I didn't ...' he said, then he jumped up and threw a punch, but the officer dodged it and his fist struck the doorframe.

He spat angrily over his left shoulder into the corridor and hissed. The officer looked at him, sighed deeply, and left. Arisa came rushing into the corridor with the axe in her hand.

'Pig! We don't spit on everything here! I'll wring you out till you piss your pants, Comrade Cast Iron Hero.'

She swung the axe so that the girl had to duck, then disappeared. The man watched her go with a look of relief.

The corridor emptied. The girl stood alone for a moment, then went back into the compartment. The man was sitting on the edge of his bed, still furious.

She didn't dare move. He calmed down little by little, burying his chin in a large hand and sighing.

'I can't stand looking at roosters like that guy. Dressed up like a whore for the Party. Guys like that are the reason we still haven't beaten the Afghans. A pansy like that is worse than those fairy Afghan fighters. I've seen on the news how those mussulmans handle their guns out in the desert. They carry them like babies. And what do our Red Army officers do? They take their cue from that bunch of throwbacks and go around wiggling their arses. If guys like me were running the war the way it should be run, we would've beaten those phoney kings in the first attack. But no, they've got to fag it up. When I was in the army, the gays got a pole up their arse. A real soldier knows what to do with a weapon. You shoot the enemy. Not between the eyes – in the gut.'

The girl had only one thought: she hated him.

They passed crumbling houses gobbled up by their gardens, villages eaten by forest, cities swallowed by the mossy taiga. The train sped east, dark brown clouds covering the sky, when suddenly in the south a little crack of the bright blue of spring appeared through a rift in the clouds. The spring sky. The train sped east and everyone waited for morning. The girl thought of travelling in the hot train across dreaded Siberia, how someone might look at that train and long for Moscow, someone who wanted to be on that very train, someone who had escaped from a camp without a rifle, without food, with nothing but wet matches in his pocket, travelling on skis stolen from a guard, a rusted knife in his pocket, someone willing to kill, willing to suffer freezing and exhaustion, willing to throw himself at life.

The girl had waited the whole dark, dense, quiet night to reach Novosibirsk. She had waited for the safety of the metropolis, waited to be able to be alone for just a few hours. The dry, unrelenting cold of Siberia sliced at her face and made her breath catch. A tuft of hair peeping out from under her knit cap frosted over instantaneously, her eyelashes clumped, her lips froze together. She walked along the platform and listened to the snow squeaking and crunching under her feet, the railway tracks popping in the cold's grip. She watched the gentle glow of the intermittently buzzing light from the lamp-posts. When she came back, cold, into the corridor of the train she met Arisa.

'Our beloved Victory engine with the red star on its forehead has given its all. If it doesn't get some time to cool down and rest, it will die, and that's not something any of us wants. We're going to let him take a breather, a few days' rest.'

The girl decided to go into town and reserve a hotel room. She could have a shower and some quiet time.

'You can't go out alone,' the man said. 'I won't let you. Novosibirsk will eat you alive. We'll go together. I'll take care of everything.'

Two hours later they were strolling towards the saffron-yellow-tinted sunrise and the centre of the frost-stiffened city. She felt the safety of the street under her feet. Snow banks as tall as a man grew on either side of the uneven pavement with paths trodden between them. They walked stiffly, gulping for air as they passed wastegrounds covered in snow, community gardens, a school, fences and garden gates crusted with snow, verandas with ice blossoms in their paned windows, a stocky woman wandering in a cloud of icy mist. There was so much snow in some places that the piles reached as far as the lights on the tops of the poles.

At the bus stop a cosily sleeping and abundantly steaming cluster of people stood waiting for the trolleybus in thin quilt jackets and steaming fur-trimmed hats with hefty felt boots on their feet. Golden-yellow light glimmered from the windows of a concrete highrise, the dogs in the courtyard howling like a pack of wolves. The wind blew open the coats of passers-by and tore apart the bittersweet song coming from the loose folds of an accordion. There was a barber's and hairdresser's on every corner. A wheelbarrow and pieces of rusty pipe jutted out from under piles of snow on a side street, a broken Czech sofa slouched on one corner covered in little drifts of wind-blown snow. They kept on walking, through an industrial city waking from an icy dream, crossed courtyards, and found the gloomiest queue in the universe among the chilling mist. They went to stand on a sheet of ice at the back of the line, the man first, the girl behind him. The front of the queue disappeared into the sooty, thick, frosty fog. A woman walked past and left an opening behind her in the mist. The people were steaming like horses. The man turned around quickly.

'We stand here suffering for no reason and don't complain. They can do whatever they want to us and we take it all humbly.'

An old man with large grey eyes and a basket full of home-made pies yelled from somewhere behind them.

'Jesus suffered, and commanded us to suffer. Deal with it.'

'All we want is an easy life. Deal with that,' a young man with a drinker's red nose roared.

'Not everybody can stand an easy life. Some destroy themselves,' the old man said tepidly, pulling the earflaps of his fur hat down tighter.

'Pure ignorance,' the red-nosed one threw back.

'Suffering is what gives life its flavour, thank God. Want and emptiness are good for you,' the old man grunted.

'It's true that a person can get by on little, but without that little, you've got nothing,' the young man shouted.

'Shithead. I won't discuss this with you,' the old man said with a sharp swing of his hand clad in a dogskin mitten.

'It's just a joke, old man. No need to get all worked up about it. Think of your heart,' the girl's companion said soothingly, his voice cordial.

The old man walked up and gave him a long, critical look.

'Listen here, comrade,' he said. 'A simple life keeps the spirit wholesome.'

'And suffering purifies,' the man answered, giving him a wink.

He bought a frozen watermelon, she bought a speckled frozen apple. They walked past a tattered phone booth where a woman with a yellow throat was speaking excitedly into the receiver. A man with red, bony ankles tapped a coin against the glass, trying to hurry her. There were deep cracks in the walls of the blocks of flats, snow-covered balconies that sagged and dripped, rows of doors hanging open, their handles stolen, an entrance filled with snow. Street lights buried in snow, extinguished, bent, broken. Electric power lines hanging in the air, open manholes, heaps of cables lying jumbled in the snow-drifts. And over it all shone an oversized sun in a clear blue sky. They made their way side by side to the dark fairgrounds. The paths had been ploughed, icy asphalt poked through the snow. They sat down on a snow-covered bench. The man took his folding knife out of his pocket, snapped open the sturdy blade, and cut up the melon.

'Shall we go for a drive? There's always time, and always will be. I've got a master plan that will cost us a bottle of whisky.

Have you got it with you? I have an acquaintance here, or rather a good friend, who can arrange things, but even in this country, not everything's free. You can wait here.'

The girl thought for a moment, dug a litre bottle of whisky out of her backpack, and handed it to him. He gave a satisfied whistle, popped the bottle into his breast pocket, and left. The girl sat on the bench shivering. Her cheeks glowed red and there were little drops of ice hanging from her nostril hairs. A crow, stiff in the morning frost, landed hard on the bench next to her. She offered it a piece of the frozen melon. The crow turned its head proudly away.

She had been fifteen when the train rattled through a Moscow neighbourhood in the early morning. She had watched from a window as the sun rose slowly from beyond the horizon over the red flags, stretching the shadows of the endless modular highrises to a surrealistic length. They were staying in the Hotel Leningradskaya on the edge of Komsomolets Square – her father, her big brother and herself. The ornate lobby of the hotel was bewildering. She had never seen such a fancy hotel, even in pictures. From the twenty-sixth floor there was a stunning view of the entire enormous city. They had full board, which meant that they could eat three times a day in the ornate hotel restaurant. She hated the black caviar, but was happy to listen to the gentle clunk of the abacus on the counter. They walked along Leningrad Prospect and watched the women street sweepers, something they'd never seen in Helsinki. In the evening they took a taxi to the Lenin Hills and looked down at her future seat of learning, the festively lit thirty-four storeys of the new Moscow University main building. Lit with floodlights, the monumental university complex and the red star on the sharp tower rising from the top of the main building looked like something borrowed from the *Thousand and One Nights*. On the second day, her father had showed her and her brother all that he had marvelled at in 1964, when he came to the Soviet Union for the first time. They walked around the functionalist Lenin Mausoleum in Red Square and admired the walls of the Kremlin. They rode the trolleybus to Uprising Square to marvel at the twenty-storey block of flats and to Smolensky Square to gape at the twenty-seven-storey office building, which their father said was a mixture of Kremlin and American skyscraper. They visited the graves of Gogol, Mayakovsky, Chekhov, and Ostrovsky at the Novodevichy Cemetery.

On the third day, her father took them to the Kosmos pavilion at the National Economic Achievement exhibition. It was a shrine to the Soviet cult of outer space: life-sized model spaceships and satellites, every sort of smaller space paraphernalia, and of course the most esteemed relic of all, the Soyuz space capsule, with a grandiose, Soviet-style flower arrangement in front of it. You weren't allowed to go inside it, but you were free to take as many photos as you liked. The pavilion was the best thing she'd ever seen in her life. She wrote in her diary that she wanted to move to Moscow as soon as she turned eighteen.

That evening they went to an Uzbek restaurant. An orchestra played Slavic songs and some people danced. At about midnight her drunken brother got into a fight with a West German tourist and someone called the militia, who came and took them both to jail until the tour guide came to bail

her glum brother out for fifty dollars the next day. Before the
restaurant had closed, her father had purchased a pretty Georgian whore, slipped away with her, and got hepatitis B as a
souvenir. The girl had been left at the restaurant by herself. A
fat waitress had called a taxi for her. She had cursed her whole
family, including her mother, who had left them years ago and
gone to northern Norway to work in a fish cannery. When her
father got back in the morning he said that the whore tasted
like milk and had a cunt as deep as sin. Moscow had been a
stony fist, like in Mayakovsky's poem. She never recovered.

A mighty sun swallowed the black clouds and a sturdy but
well-dented green Pobeda with bulging sides appeared at the
edge of the park.

'This way, my girl! Come here! Not those rusted-out
kopecks – I'm here in this beauty,' the man called from the
open window of the car.

The petrol-fumed warmth melted her frosty hair in a
moment, but the floor of the car was cold. Her toes tingled.
She took off her shoes and rubbed her frozen feet. The car
smelled like burnt leather and old iron.

The man pressed the accelerator to the floor and the Pobeda
dove into a side street strewn with chunks of ice. The sun-
yellowed, snow-covered trees in the park looked after them in
alarm.

The car zigzagged at reckless speeds through the frozen city
towards the road out of the city, past checkpoints and men
armed with machine guns, and into the bright countryside.
The icy noise of the city, the soot-blackened highrises and
slabs of smoke rising straight towards outer space were left
behind. A row of white-trunked young birches stood on either

side of the road. Bristling crows' nests grew in their branches. Fire hydrants and women wrapped in thick woollen scarves appeared at the southern ends of houses hidden by three-metre snow banks. Soon the hydrants gave way to creaking wells covered in thick ice. The man drove along the slushy, meandering, winter-rutted road as fast as the hefty car could carry them.

The car was soon bouncing along the factory-blackened Tomsk road. Snow swirled and the bridges rumbled. The transistor radio played Solovyov-Sedoy's *Unforgettable Evening* in the front seat, the man chain-smoked *mahorkkas* and took big swigs from a long moonshine bottle.

Here and there among the unbroken wall of trees trapped in banks of ice lay fields ploughed and abandoned under heavy drifts of snow. Alongside one field stood two Ladas with their front ends crumpled. The drivers were nowhere to be seen, but there was frozen blood on the ground. Something sorrowful hovered over the many bends in the road.

In the middle of a little grove of pines a frail old church jutted up unexpectedly, like a flowering shrub in the direst Siberian winter. It defied all architectural logic, looking as if its surprising proportions were derived from a toy, growing uncontrollably in every direction. Above the entrance was a sign that read *Club*.

The girl looked out of the icy, windblown rear window at Russia's wild beauty. A sparkling, violet-yellow cloud of snow covered the entire landscape as they passed, sometimes forming a wake of snow and flakes of ice that trailed behind them like a veil. A frosty field of thistles glittered and gazed darkly from the edge of the forest. Far off on the horizon a pink powdery smoke drifted, thick clouds broke up and flapped like a child's sheets in the sky.

That afternoon they passed the district capital, a pond, a *kolkhoz* farm, and a birch grove, then descended into a valley, where the sun had defeated the Siberian cold and the winding road turned slushy for a moment. The man slapped his black-mittened hands on the steering wheel. A concrete culvert was lying in the middle of the road. He hit the brakes hard and barely managed to avoid it.

'Good God, what yokels! Crooked noses, stuff falling off the backs of their trucks. Nobody pays attention to anything. They're too excited about their new tractor.'

Suddenly the sun at the edge of the grove shuddered and dived behind a greenish cloud. A moment later the first tin-heavy rain splattered against the windshield. The car had no wipers – all they could see was the stiff rain – and the man had to stop and pull over. The congealed raindrops battered the roadway into a porridge of slush. The frost-heaved road trickled through the valley like a lazy river. A one-winged crow was falling through rainbow-flaming sky.

Soon the fierce, pattering sleet and the rainbow vanished, a great green mist snaked among straight-trunked groves and gloomy swathes of forest, the sun rising bright beyond it, and a hard frost struck. The uneven road froze in an instant into crags of ice and the Pobeda bounced over it like a ping-pong ball. Beyond the hard, treeless, freezing taiga were cold, snow-buried villages, steaming *kolkhozes*, smoking government farms where mountains made entirely of black bread grew next to the barns.

As the ice-ravaged road ended, a highway trodden flat by

earth-moving machinery lay spread before them. The man hit the accelerator, then immediately braked, then accelerated again. The sun brightened the whole landscape and leapt at the next curve to light the edge of another cloud. Soon it was peeping out from behind the stiff, snow-wrapped trees. Along the edge of the road a motorcycle was half-buried in snow. The red sledge behind it was filled with snow-covered logs. The Pobeda swerved from one pothole to another, was stuck spinning its wheels for a moment on the icy shoulder, then sprang forward a few metres. The man ground the car's tortured clutch, the girl jiggled in the back seat. She was with Mitka in a sleepy museum, in the last row of a movie theatre, in the bustle of the street, in a swaying commuter train, between creaking rail carriages, staring down a skyscraper's lift shaft, on the banks of the Moscow River where trucks whined over the multi-lane shore road, at a corner table in a cocktail bar, always looking for a new place to be 'their' place. The snow-draped evergreens changed to low-growing birch. One ray of light emerged from the frozen branches, then another, and a few kilometres later a brawny sun lit up the snowy expanse.

They passed a road construction crew, swerving to avoid the machines, one of them a combination of a motorcycle and a plough, another looking like a combination of private sedan and excavator, only the steamroller looking like what it was. Hot tar boiled in large iron cauldrons, women dressed in blue cotton coats and carrying heavy stones glared angrily, men wielded long-handled shovels, cigarettes hanging from the sides of their mouths, the machines sputtering.

Beyond the construction crew were log houses. They formed a grey village at the top of a grey, slushy road. From behind the nearest house appeared a hundred-head flock of grey sheep herded by a weatherbeaten young man. He was sitting on the back of a skinny brown nag, waving a switch and cursing loudly enough to be heard from the car. Rotting sheaves of flax, rusted-through zinc buckets, broken axles, hardened sacks of fertiliser, torn birch-bark shoes and piles of rags, crazily leaning fences decorated with frost, and unconscious drunks with stray dogs peeing on them lay along the sides of the road. They parked the car in front of the general store and walked down a village lane trodden by thousands of feet. The cold stung their eyes, tears flowed down their cheeks and then froze. The man sat on an icy rock and wiped the sweat from his brow.

The girl walked to the top of a little hill behind a house. She touched the wall with her hand. It was cold but soft. A path had been shovelled from the porch to the gate, the ice chipped away around the well. At the well stood a hunched, teenaged boy with a wrinkled brow and a worn sheepskin cap balanced on his head. He watched her curiously, his mouth slightly open, his long arms hanging dumbly, his short legs apart.

'Complex brigade leader,' he said, pointing at himself with his mitten.

Soon a black horse appeared from the other side of the house pulling a red sledge. In the cart were two wooden tubs, but no driver. The boy with the wrinkled brow quickly filled them from the creaking, crackling communal well, grabbed the bridle, and took the freezing water to the farthest house.

The village houses looked at each other timidly. They were built in harmony with the surrounding nature, unpainted, melting completely into the uniform landscape. They had been built beam by beam, in uniform, rhythmic rows on either side of the village street, the fences built post by post. You could see all that, even though time had passed them by and soon nature would reconquer all of it. Where the village stood, the first few alders would grow, then the thicker, red-trunked pines, and in the end a forest of different trees. A chainsaw whined unevenly behind a shed, then sputtered and died. There was a sign fastened to the top part of the shed door: *Kolkhoz Technological Depot*. A pile of split wood stood tall next to the door and beyond it sat a crowd of boys. They had inherited too-big quilt jackets and suitcoats from their fathers, on their feet were felt boots, and they were passing around a bottle of moonshine. When it was empty, one of them slipped into the woodpile.

The man and the girl walked back to the shop. Two tractors were parked in the shop's parking area. One of them had a cab built of rough boards with a windshield made of an old screened house window. The other had loose caterpillar tracks instead of wheels and a bicycle wheel where the steering wheel had been. The girl bought some oven-fresh cabbage rolls and a bottle of compote, the man a bottle of moonshine. They sat down on the steps of the shop next to a tousled white cat. Five lively little honey bees appeared from somewhere. They buzzed around the girl's cabbage roll in the shrieking cold. When she waved them away, they flew off offended, except for one that tried to land on the branch of a rose bush and died before it touched down.

An orchestra came out from behind the shop. Sons and daughters of Siberia dressed in Pioneer uniforms marched in rhythm with a song and a little drum along the village road. The children's puny bodies were covered in loose brown shirts blown by the cold wind. Their red Pioneer kerchiefs hung prettily against their brown shirts, and multicoloured, tasselled hats shaded their open, innocent faces.

When the Pioneers had disappeared behind the schoolhouse, the man and the girl went back to the car and continued their leisurely journey.

'People used to think that God was nature, but nowadays you hear people say that God is the city. I'm in the latter camp. Some say that cities are cancerous cells. Bullshit! They say it's just common sense that a dozen worms can't eat off the same apple forever. There's enough nature here to last forever. It's free, it'll go on forever. Our supply of people is inexhaustible. We'll never run out of the masses. In the fifties, in the village of Suhoblinova, a machine-station brigadier once told me that freedom is open spaces you can walk through your whole life long, breathing the open air, filling your chest full of the breeze, feeling the endlessness of space over your head. Maybe it is. Maybe not.'

Between the hillsides wound the broad, ice-trapped, sunlit Ob River. Long, stiff, frosty grasses peeped out from between piles of snow on its banks to greet the travellers. The river wound faithfully beside them, sleeping under a thick crust of ice. They stopped often, merely out of curiosity or when the motor started to smoke.

They walked for a while on the mighty river's frozen sandbanks. The cold dry reeds rustled coarsely. The sobbing north wind carried sharp, powdery snow. The man stopped to listen to the silence.

'If some yellow-eyed wolves pop out from somewhere over there we should listen to them and answer, We're doing fine, thank you, brothers.'

There was a small current in the water near the shore. Bits of ice floated in the swirl of water. Farther off, a boat covered in the snow's deep winter dream and a birch bark hut were tumbled into the land's embrace, hibernating. Two male capercaillies crouched side by side beyond a row of winter-killed rowan trees, a few crows glided across a sky promising snow. To the north of the birds, a strange black space opened up. The man wanted to go there, to the middle of the fields of snow gnawed by early spring mists. The wind whistled over the white expanse where verdant grass grew in summer. The sun blazed orange, like a glowing ember. The dazzling snow stung their eyes. Under its icy, knife-sharp crust the snow was so fluffy, dry and soft that they sank deep with each step, up to their knees, then their thighs, then their hips, and finally as high as their navels. As they came to a clearing there was less and less snow until it turned to a smear of clay that clung to their boots.

They soon reached their destination. It was a patch of asphalt, its surface warm. The naphtha scent of the tarmac smelled like the hot summer streets of Moscow. The man sized up the spot enthusiastically.

'A space ship landed here. You can tell from the crater shape. There are landing sites like this all over Siberia, especially in Kolyma. There's about a dozen stations here where scientists study UFOs and outer space.'

As they waded sweating through the deep snow back to the road, the throb of IL-14 engines roared overhead. Farther away, at the edge of the expanse of snow huddled a lone, grey, wooden house. A birch bark Ostyak yurt had been built in front of it. The girl wanted to go there.

'The Ostyaks live like wild animals,' he warned her. 'They live poorly. Nothing works. They're a rotten people. Crooked. Liars. Every geezer you meet's named Ivan.'

They walked along a little snow path and into the drift-encircled yard. Dogs ran out to meet them, their tails wagging. The snow had been trodden away in front of the porch; they could stand there without sinking to their hips. The roof of the house was sagging, the chimney half collapsed. They stood in the brisk air as if waiting for the inhabitants to come out, then the girl climbed the rotted steps to the door and knocked. Nothing happened. They tried the door – it was unlocked. The man was turning to go back to the car when a fearless Ostyak woman with beautiful features appeared at the door and gestured something to the girl.

'She's deaf,' the man said in a weary voice.

The girl gestured towards the skilfully built yurt and then pointed to her eyes. The Ostyak woman laughed silently and nodded. She put on a large pair of rubber boots and came out of the house to escort the girl to the yurt, smiling shyly. The cold wind swept over the frozen dirt floor of the yurt. The quickening light of spring made its way in through the yurt's open door. It served as a fishing shed. Rotting, crumbling net staves, fish traps woven from bast, a small rusted milk separator and a lidless box made of planed birch full of mouldy grain.

As the girl stepped back outside, the man pulled the car up next to the yurt.

'A filthy bunch, arms half a metre long and bodies a metre, and shapeless,' he snorted, turning the car back towards the highway. 'That whore right there'd be in her element hunting rabbits. They all ought to be forced to be normal Russians, without sparing the torture, if that's what it takes. What they need is a father's iron hand!'

Silence pressed heavy on the car for a moment.

In the afternoon, when the disc of sun hung over the roofs of the highest houses, they reached the godforsaken town of Tomsk. The man drove up and down the unploughed, truck-rutted streets. The sun was fleeing purple into the far west, to the north the bashful, rose-red evening blush held still for a moment as a gritty yellow snow began to fall. The north wind battered the sides of the car. The man stopped in front of a beer house on the outskirts and left the engine running.

The girl stretched her legs in the back seat. The engine chugged and sputtered tiredly, sometimes screeching and lurching as if it were having a heart attack. The chassis shuddered, the springs squeaked. Exhaust seeped into the car and made her cough. She turned off the engine. Soon it was so cold in the car that she got out.

The door to the beer house was in constant use. An endless stream of thick-soled felt boots came and went.

When the man got back to the car reeking of yeast it was the wee hours of the morning.

'I got caught up in talking with a kid in there. One of those Samoyeds from the Taimyr district. A genuine drinking spirit.'

The wind had changed to the south and had a spring-like tune. Clumps of snow slid from the roofs of the houses and thudded onto the shovelled pavements. The man passed out in the front passenger seat with a bottle of vodka in his hand. The girl turned the ignition key. The engine grumbled angrily and died. She turned it again – it howled for a moment. She imitated the man, coaxing the engine for a long time with gentle words, then turned the key again. It squawked pathetically, but didn't die. She let it run, praising it at length before she gave it some petrol and somehow got it to move forward.

She drove Soviet style, with only the parking lights on as she moved through a city slashed with morning shimmer. A red Lada Combi stood empty at the edge of a bridge. The driver's-side door hung open obscenely, the flickering tail-lights blinking at the sky. The night's last stars trailed around the rising sun and the wind-knocked lampposts went out one by one. The girl looked at the pink blocks of flats, their narrow, loose-hanging storm windows dragged back and forth by the strong southern breeze.

The car bounced up and down over Tomsk's narrow streets. She stopped at intersections and looked into street-corner mirrors that warped and broke up the peaceful cityscape. The man dozed, drooped, started awake, drank some more vodka and perked up. The girl looked for a hotel but didn't find one. She finally parked at a bus stop. The man got out of the car and strode over to the queue of quietly waiting, sullen Soviet citizens.

'Well, my girl, first go left, then veer straight ahead like a civilised person, and finally swing in just past that dust-covered, windowless industrial complex,' he said when he got back to the car.

The factories, workshops, and warehouses of the industrial

complex were half-buried in snow; only the branching rails of the complex's own freight yard glimmered in the night. Behind it huddled a small, faded log house eaten by the earth. A yard light hung from a dangling wire, its bulb broken.

'Here it is – our hotel. Stop the car. The old biddy who lives in this dump puts travellers up for the night.'

They walked lazily arm in arm up the steps. The murk of the winter morning floated around the cabin. Next to the door hung five broken latches; the door had no handle. The girl pried it open. They were greeted in the dark entryway by a buzzing electricity meter attached to the door frame. A balalaika as big as a wardrobe nestled in the corner.

The speciality hotel was run by a dried-up old woman wearing three wool coats and two long thick brightly coloured skirts. She had a wart on her cheek with a little spike growing out of it. She lived with her three adult working sons, all of them sleeping in the kitchen so that she could rent the other two rooms to travellers.

'We need to get some sleep, granny dear,' the man said, his voice drained of all energy.

'What kind of talk is that? You'll have plenty of time to sleep in your grave. First tea, then maybe some rest.'

A piece of worn vinyl lay over the sticky wood floor of the kitchen. The floorboards cracked and squeaked. The walls were slanted, with black electrical cords meandering across them like leeches. The colour portrait of Stalin in the icon niche hung crooked and under it was an old icon of Saint Nikolai. The shelves of the doorless pantry sagged with canned and dried foods. The space between the windowpanes was crammed full of perishable food. A large enamel tub sighed in the darkest corner of the kitchen, full of pickled cabbage flavoured with lingonberries. Just outside the window was what seemed to be a vegetable garden, sleeping under piles of ashes tossed among the snowdrifts.

The old woman offered them some cabbage soup, buckwheat porridge, tea, jam, and fish pies. She had a pretty, cracked, tea set. She polished the large spoons by spitting on each one and wiping it on her clean flowered apron. The girl dozed, lost in her own thoughts. The man wiped the sweat of the beginnings of a hangover from his brow. His head fell with a clunk onto the tabletop and he started to snore. The old woman set out a cabbage pie tasting strongly of caraway and poured the girl a second cup of tepid tea nearly indistinguishable from warm water. She drank it in small, wary sips.

'When I was a little girl my father sold me for a bottle of vodka to a wrinkled old Russian man. The old geezer dragged me to this place, his house, and how I cried. As soon as he had a chance he knocked me up, but luckily he died before his son was born. So this house was left to his blind sister, me and the boy. The three of us lived quite well together. Then the blind girl died and it was just me and my son, until one mosquitoey summer day when a Samoyed walked in the door. He had beaten his old lady till she went crazy, now it was my turn. Soon enough I had another son. We lived well for a while. Just a little while.'

The old woman got up and popped over to a cupboard, took out a half-drunk bottle of vodka, and sloshed a shot into her teacup.

'He was a keen hunter but he drank up all his money. The boys and I were living on the edge of starvation. One Easter he went out on some errand and never came back. His younger brother brought me the news about his death: he'd been in a drunken fight and got a knife in his belly. The brother stayed here to live. A good man. I had three daughters and they all died. Then this brother fell in the well there next to the house and drowned. I got on as a cleaner at the factory and my life was starting to work out. As an old woman I had another son. He's out there on the river with his brothers.'

There was the sound of a mouse from behind the pantry.

'I'm so contented living in my own house, even though I've hated this Russian dump all my life.'

She got up, fetched some hardbread from the pantry, arranged it prettily on a flowered porcelain plate, and set it in front of the girl.

'The only thing I miss is the tundra.'

When the man woke up he snarled, 'The old biddy's talking pure nonsense, thinks she's some Pushkin.'

The girl's room was small, dark and dreary. The stink of ancient bedding had settled in to live there, an old Gobellin tapestry rasped against the mould-streaked wallpaper. A hot, glowing stove filled the room, but the corners of the outer walls were nevertheless covered with a thick frost and there was clear ice along the edges of the floor.

She lay on the straw mattress between two clean starched sheets. The smooth coolness of the sheets soothed her. The sun rose silently and the stars vanished from the dusty blue sky. A mouse gnawed and scratched behind the wallpaper. She fell asleep.

She woke to a cat's yawn. It had appeared next to her pillow and was staring at her without blinking. She stroked the old cat's shining coat and listened to the crackle of the frost in the corners, the clatter of the samovar, the old woman's clomping footsteps. For a moment she watched the dust float motionless against the light, then jumped out of bed in a panic and peeped out of the window into the frail morning. She'd slept through a whole day.

She picked up the cat. It opened its toothless mouth to mew, but didn't manage to get any sound out. She felt a great sadness.

She'd met Mitka at a Melodiya shop when she was in her third year of studies. He was misshapen, a stooped, four-eyed thing with a shovel beard on his chin. He had thick, short, coal-black hair and eyes that blinked as if the light were a particular strain on them. They had gone to a juice bar, talked for many hours and agreed to meet again. Mitka had liked her ice-blue eyes and thoughtless laugh. Several weeks later he invited her to his apartment. His window looked out towards a small park. She had admired the smoky mist, the city wrapped in milky fog, the pink winter sky. Mitka said he'd just turned seventeen. He had a broad old iron bed with a hard horsehair mattress, a striped linen sheet, and a white duvet with clinking bone buttons. She stayed the night. Then came other nights, other days, all the same, filled with a bustle of light and shadow.

The old woman set the table with a bowl of buckwheat porridge, a pot of steaming fatty borscht, and in front of the man a glass dish of smetana and a handsome bottle of vodka. The girl drank tea, the old woman chai. The man wiped sweat from his brow, gobbling up the smetana and, belching with satisfaction, poured another glass of vodka.

'Let's drink to the women of the world. A toast to the wisdom of the old, the intelligence of the heart, and the beauty of the young, to your friendship, dear granny, and to the silver-sided gudgeon!'

After the toast, the man wolfed down some black bread he'd spread with mustard, salt and pepper. He filled his vodka glass and stood up for a moment.

'Many a citizen has rushed ahead only to end up waiting in some awful place, so let's not rush. Let's enjoy each other's warmth, enjoy this moment.'

When it was time to leave, the man fished a slim Chinese flashlight and twenty-five roubles out of his pocket and handed them to the old woman. She nodded, satisfied, and followed them to the door. The man and the girl stepped out of the steamy hot kitchen into a fresh, frosty morning that lashed their faces like a whip.

The man wrestled the wheel of the Pobeda with heavy hands. On a small straight stretch his head knocked against the steering wheel. The girl suggested that she drive.

Gradually the belly-down, snow-filled row by row of fields changed to the notched beam by beam of a village and the village to a slushy suburb, log houses and prefab highrises side by side. The gardens and potato patches of the log houses stretched as far as the city in one direction and back to the forests and fields in the other. Then the suburb changed street by street into the muddy built-up city of Novosibirsk.

Carp were hung to dry outside the highrise windows. Grey pigeons padded along the sills, back from their winter vacations.

The man gulped back his hangover, which the glasses of

vodka hadn't managed to displace. He was shaking all over, his adam's apple shuddering.

'If I could just have a drink from a pickle jar, everything would be all right. Soothe my heart.'

His face was red and he looked so grave that the girl couldn't bear it and turned her head away.

He asked her to stop at a corner where a blue tanker truck was parked.

'I'm feeling so awful that I have to stop here and get out.'

He jumped quickly out of the car, took an empty ten-litre can out of the trunk, and went to fill it from the truck container, which had the word KVAS painted in pretty black letters on its side. When he came back to the car with the can under his arm he was humming cheerfully.

'Toothache.'

He sipped straight from the can, a hopeful look on his face. The sweet smell of kvas pervaded the whole car.

'No more toothache.'

A Gagarin smile spread across his face.

'When I fell in love with Katinka, I didn't have a single kopeck. I'd been flat broke for months, but life still had flavour, and I had plenty of food, pussy and vodka. Then there Katinka was, at the bread-shop door, and I was so drunk that I asked her to come and see me. That's when the trouble started. Now I was a fellow who had a lady visitor coming, or at least some sort of whore, a fellow who didn't have any money for *bubliks* or tea or champagne. So I rolled up my sleeves and got humming. First I asked my next-door neighbour Kolya if he'd loan me five roubles. All he had was three and he needed them himself, he honked. I tripped over to the corner room, to Vovka's place, maybe he had a rouble or two, but the old boozer was completely broke. I went downstairs to where Sergei lived and begged him for a fiver. I can give you a rouble, he said. So on I went, from door to door. Went through all my friends and enemies, and the next week I had a pile of it, twenty-six roubles and three kopecks. I could feel it all the way down to my cock. Katinka came worming her way in. I offered her champagne and I drank a few bottles of vodka. Everything was set. When it was time to go to bed, I kidded around, shy, undemanding. I got out the camp-bed and made myself a little nest, offered Katinka my bed. And then what happened? I stretched out, my head full of nothing but pussy, and Katinka grabs hold of my cock so hard the camp-bed went crashing. She glues her sweaty cunt to my dick and I let it go. And just as the whole thing's almost over she coughs up something about marriage. There I am in an ecstasy of cunt, and I say, Why not?'

He rubbed a finger over his swollen lips.

'That's not what happened. But it could have.'

They found the crooked-nosed owner of the Pobeda from a phone number kiosk squeezed between two co-op kiosks. The old man was wrapped in a frayed cotton jacket and had arms so long that they reached to his knees. The two men spoke for a moment in murmurs, then he invited them to eat.

They walked shivering to a local communal cafeteria. A sign drooped from the door: THIS FACILITY IS CLOSED. They went inside.

A greasy smell drifted from the industrial-looking kitchen. The dining room was wide and high and its utilitarian furniture was functionally arranged. There were long tables in front of the windows with long benches along either side. They went to the end of the queue that had formed at the food counter. On the main wall of the dining room was a fair reproduction of Ilya Repin's painting *Reply of the Zaporozhian Cossacks to Sultan Mehmed*. At the place on the painting where the angry letter is being written someone had used a ball-point pen to scrawl the words: *To Stalin*. A fan rattled against the back wall; under it was the carcass of a sofa covered in flowered oilcloth.

The girl chose a glass of thick tomato juice and garlic herring from the case and black bread from the counter. She scooped out a bowl of thin peasant stew with sharp bits of bone floating in it from a large pot, carried it to a table on a slimy tray, sat down and tasted the herring, but it was so heavily salted that she left it uneaten. The man slurped his soup with elaborate relish, the crooked-nosed man ate his buckwheat porridge and beets unobtrusively. When they'd finished eating, the crooked-nosed man scratched his bald head doubtfully.

'As our district professional council representative used to say in times like this, when a gypsy dreams about a pudding, he doesn't have a spoon, so he goes to bed with a spoon in his hand, and then the pudding's gone.'

The girl's travelling companion gave a bored sigh.

'By which he only meant that history dictates that happiness will eventually come to us either way.'

Her companion spat lazily on the floor.

'Women are afraid of snakes, Finns are afraid of Russians, Russians are afraid of Jews, and Jews ...'

Her companion pressed his lips together scornfully, got up from the table, and walked calmly out of the cafeteria with a slight bounce in his step.

'That fellow's a fast talker. A born flesh peddler,' the crooked-nosed man said, startled and frightened. Then he gave a long, resigned sigh. 'If I'd known that, I wouldn't have given him my car.'

The girl handed twenty-five of her companion's roubles to the crooked-nosed man. He nodded gratefully and quickly slipped the banknotes into the pocket of his quilt jacket. She got up and hurried out.

The light from a CCCP sign perched on the roof of a government building on the main street sliced through the darkness of the night. The man and the girl trudged to the station, gloomy and exhausted. It wasn't until she heard the whistle of the engines and saw the station yard with its old engines lying forever dead that her mood lightened. The familiar train, the sight of the familiar snouts of stray dogs the size of foals with their tangled coats cheered the man up as well. They stopped at the platform and listened to the train of the tsars snuffling contentedly on its tracks. As they stepped into the compartment the man whistled and sang, '*Oh Russian land! Forget your lost glory, your flag torn* ... How does it go again? ... Never mind!'

He watched her movements. He had a broad, malicious grin on his face.

'Thinking about what just happened? That was a rotten-lunged unscrupulous Jewish magpie. I won't sit at the same table with a Jew because the Jews killed the Virgin Mary.'

His words made her heart knock in her chest. She counted in her mind: one, two, three ... nine ... twelve ... until she calmed herself. The engine gave a howl and the train jerked into motion.

The plastic speakers start to play Shostakovich's Seventh Symphony and Novosibirsk is left behind. The noise of suburbs under construction, the smooth, sunny sky. Novosibirsk, the stench of rotting steel pushing in through the open compartment windows, left behind. The faint scent of pale carnations, the sturdy aroma of garlic and the acrid stink of the sweat of forced labour, left behind. Novosibirsk, mechanics, miners, industrial city of lost dreams watched over by sooty, modern, weather-maimed suburbs, the squalid carcasses of thousands of prefab buildings are left behind. The creaking gates, the lights of blind factories sweating in forty-below weather, the corpses of tortured cats near the hotel, the felt boots and brown wool trousers, the consumer cooperatives, the exhausted land, Novosibirsk is left behind. And the industrial area changes to a suburb eaten away by air pollution. Light, bright light, and the suburb changes to something else, light, darkness, a goods train rushing past, long as the sleepless night, and light, the light of a bright Siberian sky, and housing schemes, suburbs, housing schemes, in ever-thicker clusters – this is still Novosibirsk. Trucks on an unmade road, a horse and a hayrack, the Siberian taiga with a red mist hovering over it. The forest rushing wildly past, solitary, a nineteen-storey building surrounded by ravaged fields under drifts of snow. Cascading forest. This is no longer Novosibirsk. A hill, a valley, a thicket. The train shoots towards the unknown tundra and Novosibirsk collapses in a heap of stones in the distance. The train dives into nature, throbs across the snowy, empty land.

THE MORNING LIGHT WOKE HER. The man handed her a glass of tea, put a large lump of sugar in his mouth and stirred his tea with the paper-light aluminium spoon, blowing on it for a long time before taking a slurp. She looked at the landscape outside the window for a moment. There was a little log cabin painted blue, sheltered by a lone rowan tree. In front of it stood an old man with an iron bar in his hand.

'I belong to the world socialist camp. You don't. Guys like me have been in all the camps: Pioneer camps, military camps, vacation camps, work camps. They sent me on a shovel crew when I was just a boy; I requisitioned a few cement mixers and carried them off with me. I knew very well that I'd get irons around my neck for it, but still ... The worst part was before I got caught, waiting for it to happen. It was like being between Satan's cogwheels. Then when the worst happens you just think, that's life. You won't die of hunger or dropsy. The thing I remember most about all of it is the revolting smell of rotten fish.'

The cold-dimmed dawn painted the ice on a snaking little stream golden yellow. A thick mist smoked among the thickets along the shore. The frosted limbs of the willows reached delicately towards the brightly tinted purple sky. A white-flanked deer ran out of the fog. Its little tail wagged.

'My son is a born traitor. A boy ought to have heroes like the cosmonaut Aleksei Leonov or General Karbishev, the one the Nazis froze to death. But no. He has dreams of the Yazovists, wants to move to East Germany as soon as he can get enough dollars together from his stints as an errand boy to apply for a passport.'

The man seemed to collapse in a heap. A deep gloom settled over the train compartment.

'I wouldn't move to the other side if they paid me a thousand dollars. It'd be just like moving a bird from one cage to another. I love this country. America is a God-forsaken dump.'

The sun sat balanced atop the airy forest landscape. The gloom in the compartment dispersed.

'At home in Moscow I read the newspaper out loud to Katinka and in Ulan Bator I read it to my workmates. Is it all right if I read? It's a comfort to me. However slight.'

She nodded.

'Pile-up on Moscow ring road – five dead and twenty injured; coal mine explosion in Ukraine – three hundred dead; oil rig failure in Chelyabinsk – fifteen hundred reindeer drowned in oil; funicular crumbles in Georgia – thirty-four people dead; another sunk submarine in the Arctic Ocean – seventy-one sailors dead; boiler explosion in an old folks' home – one hundred and twenty-seven dead; radiator rupture in a kindergarten – forty-four children sprayed with boiling water; passenger boat sunk in the Black Sea – two hundred and six passengers drowned; chemical plant cancels work contract – an entire town wiped off the map; hydroelectric dam collapses in Karelia – thirteen villages underwater and seven hundred people drowned; if a power plant were to break down, a million people would die of radiation sickness.'

He paused and waited.

Straightened his back, turned the page, and took a breath.

'Soviet pilots lost five cruise missiles on a test flight over Sahkalin Island. That's what it actually says here.'

He flung the paper under his bed and examined the window frame for a long time.

'I was in school, maybe in the sixth year. I had a classmate named Grigor Mityakovich Kozinichev. And then there was this talentless teacher, Yarek Koncharov Ust-Kut. Comrade Ust-Kut.' He burst out laughing. 'What kind of a name is that? We laughed about it even then. For some reason this Comrade Ust-Kut hated Grigor. Tormented him almost every day. Sent him to the front of the class, cuffed his ears and face, yelled at him, called him stupid. We'd think, Not again! And then he would do it again. But one day Grigor grabbed the pointer and swung it at Comrade Ust-Kut's face, then threw it on the floor and ran out of the door. This caused quite an uproar. The janitor came in, the principal and the other teachers all agog. The stupid prick just had a little scratch next to his nose and the lesson continued. Then, just before the minute hand clicked to breaktime, the door opened and there stood Grigor Mityakovich Kozinichev in the doorway, and he had a real gun in his hand. He aimed it at Comrade Ust-Kut, and when the comrade realised what was happening, he started to squeal like a pig. Then Grigor shot him. The blood flowed and the creep died. Grigor could very well have shot me or any prick there who'd been bullying him the whole year. But no. He spared us. Back then I didn't understand yet that the only kind of people you should kill are the ones who are afraid of death. Otherwise you're just doing them a favour.'

The train crawled forward, as if asking pardon. The sun rose whole in the milk-white sky and lit up the pure white snow.

It continued proud for several hours, then was covered by a black darkness for a moment. Siberia disappeared outside the window, then slipped back before anyone could even notice. A wall of forest grew, black and frightening, right next to the tracks. When it had finished, a broad view opened up as far as the river. On the open sea of snow were three houses with a smoke sauna in front of them gushing black smoke. Outside the sauna, surrounded by a cloud of steam, stood a fat naked woman, red and barefoot. The man offered the girl some Pushkin chocolate. It was dark and peppery.

He glanced out of the window and caught a glimpse of the woman.

'Weak design, but well sewn together.'

The girl smudged and scribbled for a long time before she drew the Siberian village in its endless landscape. The man stared at her, his mouth slightly open.

'This fellow named Kolya had a joke he used to tell: Guys like us in the army grow iron jaws, iron cheekbones, and an iron will. But the welds between them are such crap that when we get back to civilian life the whole contraption falls apart until the only thing that'll help is a metre and a half of dirt.'

He broke into such a chuckle at this that he had to wipe his eyes with his sleeve. He knelt on the floor, picked the torn newspaper up from under his bunk, folded it neatly, and slipped it under his mattress.

'This other fellow named Kolya whose hopes hadn't come to fruition painted a red sign with white lettering that asked: What's taking our happy future so long? He took the sign with him and stood on Red Square. He managed to stand there for about three minutes before the militia showed up and took him away. They slapped a twenty-six-year sentence on him, the same time our forefathers spent in the army. And he lost his citizenship rights for five years. What's taking our happy future so long! Even the pigeons in Red Square laughed at that.'

A fire-red afternoon sun spread over the wind-whipped sky. Behind it dripped vast sheets of sleet. The girl rummaged in her knapsack, the man set the table for dinner. They ate slowly and silently, drinking well-steeped tea – black, Indian Elephant tea she'd bought at the foreign exchange shop. After the meal the man would have liked to talk but she wanted to be quiet. He took his knife out from under his pillow and started to scratch the back of his ear with it. She rested with her eyes closed. And that's how they travelled that whole long twilit evening, each of them sleeping and waking in their own time. She was with Mitka in his room. A Jefferson Airplane song wobbled out from the little blue record player, Mitka flipped through an encyclopaedia from the early part of the century, she lounged on the bed and copied out ancient Egyptian hieroglyphs, Zahar was in the kitchen humming an old Russian romance and peeling potatoes, and Irina was talking very quietly with Julia in the living room.

The swampy landscape silently turned to flat, level land – broken ruins of foundations buried under Siberian snow, caved-in wells, nest boxes hanging from birch trunks, villages where the dead eyes of abandoned houses stared back at the train. A caterpillar-tracked truck extinguished in a pile of snow, a horse wading through a field, its back sagging like an old sofa, pulling a feed rack behind it with two buzzards balanced there instead of hay, stiff with cold, their legs tied together.

'My friend, do you know what today is? It's Cosmonautics Day. And that's not all. Today is both Cosmonautics Day and the day that our great leader strode into heaven. The Fifth of April. All of us remember that it was the Fifth of April 1953 … no wait, it was the Fifth of March … when Generalissimo Josif Vissarionovich Stalin's valiant heart made such a fierce protest that only hours later the funerary machine roared into motion. Josif Vissarionovich, that great engineer on the train of history, was a man of such terrible and steely wisdom that he still terrifies. Let's celebrate Stalin's death, my girl, even if we are a month late.'

He started furiously rummaging in his bag, digging around and trying to calm himself.

'It must be here somewhere, it must be. It's a bottle of vodka, not a needle, and we're not in a haystack.'

He didn't find the bottle in his bag. It was under his mattress.

He splashed a generous shot into both tea glasses, pushed her glass in front of her, and lifted his own.

'Let's drink to cosmonautics.'

He filled his glass again.

'Another toast, to the wonderful young woman in our compartment, and to all the other mummified women of Finland. To beauty.'

He filled his glass again and put an official Soviet look on his face.

'This next toast is to that rabble-rouser, that great figure of world history, the Soviet Union's great departed leader, the iron papa, the bank robber of Tblisi, the Georgian Jew and the king of the cut-throats, Josif Vissarionovich Stalin.'

He tipped his glass and emptied it, took a bite of black bread, and filled his glass again.

'Let's make another toast. Let's raise our glasses again to the Man of Steel. Thank you Josif Vissarionovich Stalin for making the Soviet Union a strong industrial superpower, for sustaining hope for a better tomorrow and a gradual lessening of human suffering. With a stick in the eye for those who remember the past, and in both eyes for those who forget it … And a toast to General Zhokov, the king of Berlin. Without him the Nazis would have turned Moscow into a lit-up artificial lake and purged the earth of Slavs and other unhygienic peoples, including the Finns.'

He tipped his glass, emptied it, and splashed in one more dribble of vodka.

'The Jews poured poison in the Great Leader's mouth, and although I hate the Jews, I'll raise a toast to them for that beautiful gesture.'

He drank his glass to the bottom and tossed a weightless grin at the window.

'I remember very well the day that butcher and punisher of the peasants died. I was with Petya in the third year. In school number five. There was no number one or number four. School number one had caved in in the middle of the school day and they stopped building number four before it was finished. One morning when we got to school, our teacher, Valentina Zaitseva, said that the father of all the people was sick. That information didn't really touch a child's heart. The next morning the teacher told us that the Generalissimo was lying unconscious and the doctors said there was very little hope for him. So what? We went on playing. On the third morning she sobbed and said that Papa was dead. Some bright mind asked what he had died of. She answered that when a person holds onto life too fiercely his breathing will stop and he'll die of suffocation … I walked home with Petya, our arms around each other's necks, the factory whistles howling like ships in distress, some of the men on the street crying, others smiling. When I got home there was something odd about my grandfather, something naked and strange. I looked at him for a long time before I realised that the southern whiskers were missing from his fat upper lip. Now a new life begins, he said, and gave us some *bubliks*. He was a Party member and one of his favourite sayings was that during Stalin's time this country was the most dangerous, unhealthy place in the world for a communist to live.'

He rubbed his chin for a moment. 'There are thousands and thousands of truths. Every fellow has his own. How many times have I cursed this country, but where would I be without it? I love this country.'

The acrid smell of kerosene floated through the compartment. It came from the full vodka glass trembling on the table in rhythm to the rumble of the train. The girl pushed it aside. The man followed the jiggling glass with his eyes.

'Foreigner, you offend me deeply when you don't drink with me.'

He bit off a piece of pickle and stared at her with a cutting look in his eyes. She scowled at him and turned her gaze towards the floor.

'My mother always gave me vodka when I was sick. I was used to the taste of vodka when I was still a baby. I don't drink because I'm unhappy or because I want to be even more unhappy. I drink because the serpent inside me is shouting for more vodka.'

They sat in thought, not looking at each other. The girl thought about her father and the day she told him she was going to study in Moscow. He had looked at her for a long time with a frightened expression on his face, and then a tear had slid down his cheek. He got blind drunk, barricaded himself in his Lada, and insisted she let him take her to the station.

'I've been sitting here thinking, I wonder if God is Russian. If he is, then that would mean Jesus was Russian, too, because he's God's son. And what about Mary? How do you count her? Maybe there weren't really any Russians before Ivan the Terrible. But when he took up the sabre, heads started to roll. The people were displaced, exiled, destroyed. It's God's commandment, roared Uncle Ivan. He backed everything up with God, the fox. He even established the old-time KGB to take care of his purges. Then came Peter the Great who wanted to make us Europeans and built St Petersburg with slave labour. To please you Finns! He licked your arses. A pansy. After that came the German princess, Catherine the Great. That hag had a cunt as big as a wash tub, made Potemkin fuck her, 'cause she heard he was hung like an aubergine. There's no triumph of reason in Russian history. And what about Nicholas the First? Gave every slob a couple of hundred lashes, and a thousand runs through the gauntlet just to be on the safe side. A lot of them didn't live through that hell. We've always known the noble art of torture.'

He pressed his head against the cold glass of the window and shut his eyes. She thought for a moment that he'd fallen asleep, but he soon opened them again. A slash of orange sky flashed in the window. He looked at her tenderly.

'It's time, high time, Ivan the Terrible said, and gave the order to build the Trans-Siberian railway. Or was that Alexander the Second? Without this damned railway I could be lying around in Moscow with my honeybun in my arms. They made the railway like this to torture the poor. It could head straight to its destination in one go, but no, they have to take a piss at every godforsaken village and there are plenty of them in the Soviet countries. But on the other hand, what do I care? It could be worse. After all, we have plenty of time.'

He got up from the bed with a look of apathy on his face. He groaned, shyly put on some lighter clothes, did a couple of drunken calisthenics, sat down on the edge of the bed, and stared at the floor.

'I work for the Mongols, bringing some good to a country where my people don't live. It's not snow that falls in Mongolia, it's gravel. There are no thick forests there like we have, not a single mushroom or berry. Last year this thing happened on the job site that made every man there shit his pants. There was a comrade – let's call him Kolya. He was a shithead, but one of us. And then a herd of those mongoloids came to the site and claimed that Kolya had knifed one of them. We told 'em, Get out of here, Russians don't knife people. When we got to the site the next morning there was a wooden cross at the gate stuck into the ground the wrong way. That was neither here nor there, but on that cross hung Kolya, with his head hanging down. They had crucified him and poured hot tin down his throat. That's the kind of friends those Mongols are. Their souls are as dirty as ours, though not as sorrowful.'

The train switched gears with a jerk and stopped as if it had hit a wall. They were in Achinsk. Arisa shouted that the train would be stopping for two hours. The man didn't want to get off – the fresh air would just clear his head.

The girl jumped onto the platform and headed into a town dozing through its evening chores. She walked along the life-less boulevard towards the town centre. A heavy sleet was falling. The city was dim and shapeless, damp, silver-grey, the white moon peeping out from a straggling carpet of curly clouds that hung over the colourful houses. She stopped to look in a delicatessen display window. It was like something by Rodchenko, the packages of vermicelli lunging for the sky like lightning. She felt something warm on her foot. A small stray dog was peeing on her shoe.

The dog looked at her with sweet button eyes and barked, revealing a gold tooth. It took a few steps, then stopped and stared at her. She could see that it wanted her to follow.

They walked along the deserted street. She couldn't hear the sound of her own footsteps though the sleet was quickly changing to a snowfall that made its way lazily along Petrovskiy Boulevard, turned into a narrow side street, lost its strength as it reached a corner bread shop, and dried up. The cold tightened around her. The dog stopped and stood at a cellar window. The window opened and she heard a raspy voice.

'How many?'

She thought for a moment.

'You want two? Give Sharik three roubles.'

She took a banknote out of her pocket and, after a moment's hesitation, handed it to the dog. The dog snapped the note up in its mouth and slipped quickly in through the window. A moment later two unlabelled liquor bottles and a quarter-rouble coin appeared on the windowsill. She picked them up, thanked the empty space, and walked along the clinking, snowy asphalt back to the train. When she got there, she handed the bottles to her startled companion.

He put the bottles into a special vodka compartment in his bag, humming, and went to sleep. When he'd slept off the worst of his blind drunk, he started to arrange some supper on the table.

After they'd enjoyed a long, lazy meal, he opened the compartment door.

'Let the world in.'

He rubbed his temples and pinched his earlobes. Though she was tired, the girl worked on a sketch of the Siberian colonial town.

He wanted to see the drawing. He looked at it for a long time.

'This is nothing,' he said, tossing it back to her. 'You don't have any imagination, my girl. First you should draw a little river and then a pretty little bridge going over it. Over the bridge, on the other side of the river, you should draw a path that disappears into the tall grass, then a meadow beyond that, and then a forest. Along the edge of the forest you draw the glowing embers of a spent campfire. And last of all you streak the horizon with the last rays of sunset. That's the kind of picture I could put up on the barracks wall.'

KRASNOYARSK LOOKED ENORMOUS AS they approached from the west. It spread out over the fields, trees, and ravines. It dried up the lakes and whittled the Ice Age stones smooth as it headed east. It tore villages to the ground and begat concrete skyscrapers. The forest of plump trees was logged off, the logged-off land became a construction site, the construction site a suburb, and the suburb fused with the city.

An icy wind raced over the low land, whirled and sent the smoke from the factory chimneys flying. The tracks branched off ever more thickly. The train jerked softly at the switches, the carriage couplings squeaked, the whole machine screeched. Finally a long, gentle braking. They were in Krasnoyarsk, a closed city, a centre of Soviet arms manufacture. It started to snow. Women in grey felt boots stopped their work cleaning the tracks and stared at the train arriving from far-off Moscow. They heard Arisa's voice in the corridor.

'No one gets off at this station!'

'A peculiar city,' the man said. 'A prison for experts. But they do get a vacation.'

The compartment door opened. A woman the size of a newspaper stand whom the girl had never seen before glanced at her angrily and then huffed at the man.

'I've been listening to your disgusting talk day after day. You belong in a mental hospital.'

The man looked out the window and puckered his chin.

The woman laughed scornfully. 'I...'

'Shut your trap, lard factory!'

The woman jumped in fright and took a step backwards. 'Shame on you!' she said.

The girl escaped past her into the corridor. The white curtains of the corridor window fluttered. The man pushed the woman out of the compartment like he would a cow.

Arisa watched the situation intently from afar before squawking at him, 'I have half a mind to wrap your legs around your necks, the both of you!'

As the train slubbed into motion, a buzzard shot off with a shriek from the roof of a spent engine on the next track. It rose up in the bright moonlight and hovered under a cloud of green. A fleet of planes soared across the blue of the horizon over the round towers of the arms factory. The planes roared towards the centre of the city, broke the sound barrier, and disappeared into the sea of tall buildings. The train filled with the dark smell of hot metal.

The man said he was going to see if the dining car was open, and quickly returned.

'Nothing fucking there except an old slut with an arse like a cement mixer.'

His cheeks twitched with anger. He had a disappointed look on his face, with a hint of depression behind it. They sat all day in silence, until the purple light of night. Then he opened a bottle, poured a glass down his throat, and said in a hoarse voice:

'I love vodka, like all of my kind. Once I get going I can drink seven bottles a day. I always drink to the bottom of the bottle. Then Katinka comes with a broom in her hand to fetch me home. A week later I'm a decent man again and I go out and drink on the construction site. In addition to all the drinking I do on the job, I seem able to achieve minimum results in maximum time. If I don't have vodka I throw a fit.'

The girl was tired. She would have liked to sleep.

'How do they drink where you come from? You probably live Baltic style. The men revolve around the bottle, the women around the men, and the children around the women. It's the bottle makes everything go round. It's the opposite here. We turn the bottle, it doesn't turn us.'

She looked at him. She didn't seem impressed. His face turned stony and he looked at her sternly. 'I ain't interested in your opinions. You're just shitwater to me.'

They sat quietly. The girl swallowed.

'Forgive an idiot, my girl,' he said with genuine regret in his voice.

She turned to look out of the window. The silent moonlit Yenisei River drifted by. It split Krasnoyarsk in two. Ice fishers, gulls and crows sat on the frozen crust of the river; barges and tugboats lolled on shore, embedded in ice. Dim, distant stars seemed to sleep on its surface.

When the river was left behind, the girl went into the corridor. A hint of spring wind drifted through the train; you could smell it even through the window. A light, silent snow was falling, flakes drifting in great tufts onto the frozen ground. Without warning the train braked sharply, the wheels rumbled, the carriages lurched, soft snow came whirling up from the railbed, and a woman somewhere screamed. The girl hit her head on the window frame and it started to bleed. Arisa shouted from the the end of the passageway in a low, grating voice: 'Citizens, we are in Taishet. From here the distance to

Moscow is four thousand five hundred and fifteen kilometres and it is five hours later than Moscow time.'

The girl went back to the compartment, holding her head. The man was picking up shards of a tea glass from the floor.

He washed the cut on her forehead with vodka, blew her hair away from the wound, and put the bandage she handed him over it. The dirty air of the compartment made her feel sick. She picked up his empty water can and hurried out. The air outside was sharp and smelled of kerosene. The moon escaped behind a red cloud. She circled around the engine. On the next track was an engine that had breathed its last, lying on its side. She hurried past it and found the window of her own compartment. She set the can on the ground, put one foot on it, and wiped the window clean with a dirty sock. When she had finished she went back to the platform and boarded the train again.

The man was in a deep sleep, wheezing like a barrel of moonshine. The girl fell asleep, and when she woke to a new morning she ate breakfast quickly. The man woke up a couple of hours later. His hand moved, then one finger, then one eye. His tongue licked at his lips. A twitch. A stretch. He jumped up lazily, put on a tracksuit, did his calisthenics, and prepared himself a large meal.

They sat until evening. She drew, listened to music, ate, drew again. He dozed, played endless hands of solitaire, and dozed again.

After a lazy silence that lasted from noon to dinnertime, the man suggested that they go to the dining car for something to eat.

'You should eat in the dining car at least once on the Siberian railway. That's what it's for, and it's even open.'

The girl put on a brown wool dress that she'd not yet worn even once. The man took off his tracksuit and pulled on some polyester pants and a short-sleeved white shirt, took a round mirror out of his bag and set it in the middle of the table, and spent a long time carefully combing his coarse thick hair.

The dining car was full. Travellers were using their elbows to get a seat for themselves. The man rudely shoved his way to a white-clothed table where a feisty-looking couple were just finishing their meal. The man's beard was a carefully groomed square, the woman's grew freely. On every table rested a crystal vase full of short pink plastic carnations. The man and the couple started an odd, jumpy conversation that included something about Petrovka … Chipok … Zamoskvorestye … Varvarka … Solyanoi Dvor … Trubnaya … Kuznetsky Most.

The girl closed her ears to the noise, traced the broad windows with her eyes, and thought about a summer morning at the lake. A tired waiter arrived at the table.

'Be so good as to bring the young lady a bottle of Senator and a bottle of vodka for me, and a plate of vobla.'

'There isn't any vodka,' the waiter said sourly.

'Why is that?'

'Prohibition.'

'Rules are made to be broken,' the man said hopefully.

'There isn't any vodka,' the waiter said gruffly. 'Is that so hard to understand, comrade?'

'Bring me a bottle of cognac, then. Cognac will do nicely.'

When he'd got his plate of vobla and his cognac he took a long swig, grinned, and bit off some of the dry fish.

'Now we can order some food,' he said.

The waiter looked at him wearily.

'A bowl of selyanka to start with. For the main dish fifteen blinis, shashlik, some boiled tea sausage, salad, and a bottle of cognac.'

Instead of shashlik they got some dry chicken legs and instead of salad some potatoes fried in margarine. The man poured himself a glass of cognac, blew on the top of the bottle as if it were foamy, and said that in Brezhnev's day two hundred and fifty grams of vodka was considered a single serving.

The girl glanced at the whiskered woman and listened to her square-bearded husband for a moment.

'In my case the war only lasted five years and we all knew what to aim at, but our marriage has lasted twenty-nine years and I never know what direction an attack's going to come from …'

The girl soothed herself. What you don't remember ceases to exist. Maybe it never did exist.

Her travelling companion filled the square-bearded man's glass and slapped him on the back. Then he said it was time they went back to their compartment. He grabbed the rest of the cognac on the way out.

'I don't need a reason to drink, but I never drink alone. We Russians always booze in groups. It's more fun that way. A man has to suffer, so a man has to drink. Like I'm doing now.'

He took out the bottle of moonshine she'd given him and set it in the middle of the table. He stared at it for a long time with a vexed look on his face.

'And you, my girl, force me to drink alone.'

He wiped the side of the bottle, set it next to the half-full bottle of cognac, and looked at her with slack curiosity.

'I lived entirely without money from 1961 to 1964. I didn't have a fraction of a kopeck, but I still lived. That's possible here. You can always suck on grass roots or pick the snails off trees, and you can always find vodka. A pig will always find a wallow, as we like to say. It's harder in the winter. You suck on pine cones and gnaw at tree bark. The nice thing about vodka is that it doesn't freeze even in the bitterest cold.'

He poured his glass full, took a gulp, and quickly bit off a mouthful of green onion, grunting to himself and glancing at her tensely, an amused look on his face.

'Are all Finnish women as dry and cold as you? Russian women are the kind of whores that once you've fucked them they start farting. I know you're not like that.'

When he'd emptied the cognac he wheezed heavily, pointed at the bottle that had no label, and said in a muddy voice, 'Splitting headache. Ought to drink this one, too.'

The girl withdrew into the corridor. The train rattled steadily onward. An old man stood on the roof of a crooked house next to the tracks shovelling snow. A rusty stream wound from behind the house through the expanse of white and disappeared into the darkness of the limp eternal forest. The rugged forest would soon swallow up everything. Someone was yanking roughly on an accordion at the other end of the carriage. The clatter of the train and the sharp, slashing, Slavic sounds of the accordion sent her into a liberating torpor. She imagined the winter landscape as summer, saw a lemon-yellow meadow, a forest's hot, shimmering outline, birches reddened by a setting sun, cool, dark shadows of fields, a little billowing cloud.

She went eventually, reluctantly, again to the door of the

compartment and opened it warily. The man was lying in his own bunk like a corpse.

She tiptoed to her bed and sat down. The air was damp, the constantly brewing tea had steamed up the compartment, made the air heavy. A thick string of slobber oozed from the side of the man's mouth. His face was tranquil, as if he had forgiven every sorrow he'd had in life. She undressed and got into her bunk, beloved from use. She thought of Mitka, how he cut open an apple with his bone-handled knife and handed her half. Mitka, who smelled of soap and grass. Mitka, who was listless and lazy, but a good swimmer and a chess champion at school.

And the day faded into dusk, and the dark of night froze into the blue of dawn in the window. A yellow moon swept away the last morning star as it made way for a fiery sun. A new day was before them. All of Siberia slowly brightened. The man in his blue tracksuit bottoms and white shirt did push-ups between the bunks, sleep in his eyes, his mouth dry and smelly, the mucousy smell of sleep in the compartment, no breath from the window, tea glasses quietly on the table, crumbs silent on the floor. A new day. Yellow, frosty birches, pine groves, animals busy in their branches, a fresh snow billowing over the plains. Flapping white longjohns, limp penises, mitts and muffs and cuffs and flowered flannel nightgowns, shawls and wool socks and straggly toothbrushes. The night speeds through the dark into dim morning, a dogged queue at the shrine of the WC, a dry wash among the stench of pee, sputum, shame, sheepish looks, steaming tea glasses, large flat cubes of Cuban sugar, paper-light spoons, black bread, Viola cheese, sliced tomatoes and onion, roasted torso of young chicken, canned horseradish, hard-boiled eggs, salt pickles, a jar of mayonnaise, a tin of fish.

Night escapes into a new day. Snow rises from the ground up the tree trunks, the silence fading in their upper branches, a hawk perched on an orange cloud, looking down at the slithering worm of train.

THE RAILS TANGLED, the train rocked wildly, then a screech of brakes like glass scraping against sheet metal. The train stopped in Siberia's capital, at Irkutsk station. It spent two days there.

The yellow-ochre, white-cornered station building stood barren in its accustomed spot. In front of it the stationmaster stood, stock still, watching the train arrive. The girl turned over on her side and was assaulted by disconnected memories and impressions, people she hadn't seen in ten years. When she woke up she was wet with sweat.

The man looked at her compassionately and it felt good to her. 'Another person's soul is a dark chasm,' he said quietly. 'But let the soul be. Let's go hunting. Hunting for food!'

She dressed quickly, he slowly, with a sort of dignity. He put on an old greenish suit coat, buttoned it tightly, combed his hair back like a dandy. Last, he pulled his shoes out from under his bunk. They were some kind of fur-lined, sturdily made army boots with split tops and hard-edged heels.

They were met on the platform by a mild spring chill, silent snowflakes, and an old dog with a large femur dangling from its mouth, its tail wagging.

It was warm and dry inside the station. Glum travellers loitered in the corners, drifters sat on wooden benches in heavy winter clothes. A quiet hum of talk trickled from the people on the benches. At one end of the station was a café with a round window in the far wall, the winter light pressing through it like raindrops into the samovar-steamed air.

They came out through a low side door. They found the vendors next to the wall of the station among the frost-heaved pavement. The man greeted the old women with a wave of his hand but chose to approach an old man with a brimless cap on his head. The codger's table was covered in dried mushrooms. The man chatted with him for a moment and then handed him a set of socket wrenches made in China. The older man examined them for a long time before he reached under the table and took out a few cured Baikal salmon and a box of grilled whitefish.

Next they went to the table of a woman in a black scarf. Behind her was a smoking rotisserie of pure white, poorly plucked chicken carcasses. All she was selling was three eggs.

The man counted out a pile of one-, two- and three-kopeck coins into her hand.

They lurked among the vendors a little longer. There was a familiar smell, a combination of garlic, vodka, and sweat. The man bought some tea grown in Irkutsk, sour milk tarts, pretzels and sugared *bubliks,* the girl bought biscuits from Tula, Gold Label biscuits, and *pryanikis.*

They went over the footbridge. The airy early spring sun tinged the powdery new-fallen snow with pink, and Irkutsk seemed like a whole city in miniature made of marzipan. The air was sharp and thin; the man was panting. A flock of sparrows flew over their heads, their wings whistling. The man and the girl stood quietly for a long time. By the permanently closed back door of the station a pile of waste was covered in bright white powdery snow where a couple of dozen filthy stray cats capered about. A well-fed owl perched on a rotting cross of wood left on the rubbish heap and followed their movements closely. They walked to the kiosks. The snow glittered on the kiosk roofs and around the bottoms of the lampposts. The girl took off her cap and let her hair fall over her shoulders. She joined the long, cheery queue formed between two railings for the tobacco stand and the man joined the talkative and argumentative queue for newspapers. He bought a *Pravda* and a *Literaturnaya Gazeta*. With the change he bought a piece of rock-hard Lolek chewing gum, made in the DDR. After lengthy negotiations, the girl managed to purchase a pack of Primas and some Baikal *papirosas*. The vendor refused to sell her any Belomorkanals for some reason, although there was a whole shelf full of them. When she gave the Primas to the man he turned them over in his hand for a moment, looking at the spacecraft on the package.

'Baikals smell like dog piss. Primas taste like horse shit and Brezhnev. Belomorkanals, on the other hand, smell like the real Papa Stalin.'

They walked along the station platform back towards their compartment. A few light spring snowflakes mixed with the smell of smoke in the air. The girl looked up and let the snow fall on her face. The man stared back at the kiosks.

'I've never seen a Georgian standing in a queue before. Now I've seen everything.'

They were just finishing cleaning the train carriage. The carriage staff had taken out the carpets; Sonechka vacuumed the canvas-covered floor and Arisa cleaned the WC and wiped the doorknobs and corridor railing with a wet black cloth. The man and the girl slipped into the compartment once Arisa and Sonechka had put the carpet back in place. They spread some of their purchases on the table and started preparing breakfast together.

The man bustled over his samovar. He moved it around unnecessarily, opened the lid and checked several times to make sure the cord was plugged tight into the wall. The sun smoked beyond the rail yard, the universe hummed. He boiled some water, dumped in a mighty portion of the large whole tea leaves he'd bought, and waited. Ten minutes later the tea had sunk to the bottom of the pot. He poured the nearly black tea into his own glass, put in a whole sugar cube like an iceberg, and took three small sips. Then he handed the glass to the girl. She tasted it. It was strong and mellow. He wanted the glass back, slurped at it three times, and handed it to her again.

'My grandfather was sent to a prison camp in 1931. He was a true thief and kept the secret of the seven seals till the day he died. My father lived the life of a wanderer too, had no possessions but his poor handwriting. He lived in a world where the tavern is your church, the work camp is your monastery, and drinking is the highest form of endeavour. He got nabbed for an honest robbery and murder, and Lucifer's net closed around him. He ended up in a KGB cellar, then they tossed him into a three-star work camp in 1935, the same year Stalin announced that the life of the Soviet people was happier now. A three-star camp. In other words, a good one. He got sentenced to forty-five years. In those days life in a work camp may have been safer and more bearable for somebody poor and hungry than life in a big city. The old man wasn't afraid of being sentenced to labour because he was used to even worse. In 1941 Stalin was in deep shit. The Nazis were thirty kilometres from Red Square and their reconnaissance planes were already over Stalingrad. Then the Generalissimo, panicked as he was, decided to finally free any criminal in the work camps who would pledge to go to the front to defend his homeland. Go to the front and you'll be forgiven and after the war you'll be a free man. My old man took the bait and they freed him, like tens of thousands of others. All those killers, thieves and other crooks crammed onto prison trains and were carried to the front. It was on that trip, on one leg of the journey, that my father saw my virgin mother, who was in a great hurry to get herself pregnant before every last man was sent to the war, and had a screw when she got the chance, naturally. My old man survived the war, but after the war all those criminals who managed to stay alive on the front were thrown right back into the work camps. The only thing different was that the camps were full of Lithuanians now. That's where he died, from fever and diarrhoea.'

He licked his dry lips and looked at the girl pityingly. 'It's fun to tell you stories, my girl, because you don't understand a thing. My mother birthed herself a new man.'

He got up and expertly executed fifty-three push-ups. His legs were beautifully muscular and he had strong, firm buttocks.

'Life prescribes strict rules for all of us. You'll understand someday. Or maybe not. I was in a Pioneer camp in 1948, right after the war. The boys in the sixth section got to swim in the clear waters of Lake Komsomol. This lake was unusual because the soft sand on the bottom had sudden drop-offs, and there were some of the boys of course who thought it was funny to push the ones who couldn't swim into the cold, deep water. Little Pioneers like me swam in pond number six. It was a muddy little Pioneer pond with water that was cloudy and too warm. One day when we were splashing in it we heard a terrible boom. It came from really close by. Somebody yelled for help and we saw that there was a great fuss on the shore. We ran right over, of course, to see what it was all about. A tight, noisy circle of people had formed on the sand. I tried to get through it so I could see what was happening, but the older boys shoved me away. Then the gorilla of a camp director came and pushed his way into the middle of the action and in the fracas I managed to slip inside the circle. And what did I see? Jura was lying there, with one leg missing. He was just trembling, no sound coming out of his mouth. The director ordered us to disperse. Someone ran to get the camp truck and another director came with some bandages. The gorilla gave Jura some vodka and used it to rinse off the stump of his leg too. Then the truck came and took him away. The next day nobody said a word about it. The boys had found a mine on the bottom of the lake and thrown it on the shore, where Jura, their little whipping boy, was building a sandcastle. Thanks, Comrade Stalin, for the happy childhood!'

Pallid light poured from the sky. The girl decided to go into town alone. The man stayed on the train to rest. He too wanted to be alone.

SHE LISTENED TO THE BIRDS' spring silence, the swish of melting snow on roofs, the patter of the dripping drain spouts, the little streams trickling across wet courtyards, the sad peeping of a sparrow on a snowy rowan branch. Two-metre icicles grew from the eaves of a warped-walled highrise. There were a few parked cars along the roads, some covered in a soft blanket of fresh fallen snow, others coated in a matte finish of thick frost. A working woman sat at the bus stop with loaves of bread piled in her lap.

In the afternoon the girl sat in a cocktail bar called Great October. The place was full of students arriving and leaving, puffs of frost coming in through the door. She tried a milk cocktail made popular by Premier Kosygin that had spread from the Baltic across the Soviet Union. It was cold and sweet. She glanced at the rusted padlock on the refrigerator door and thought about Moscow, its damp courtyards, the swampy smell of the apartments, the stairwells full of different kinds of doorbells. She had gone to study at Helsinki University as soon as she finished her matriculation exam and she and her friends Maria and Anna had started applying for graduate study positions in Moscow. It took a lot of arranging. Maria and Anna moved into the conservatory dorms, she into the student house at the Teknikum. She had shared a small hot room with a Dane named Lene. Lene studied geology and she studied archaeology.

From her earliest years of study she had dreamed of how she would follow in the footsteps of Sakari Pälsi, G. J. Ramstedt, and Kai Donner, seek out the same holy sites where those scholars had been. When her thesis was nearly finished she started to fill out requests and applications and gather authorisations, endorsements, and letters of recommendation from Helsinki and Moscow. All her efforts were in vain; those regions were closed to foreigners. Finally Mitka suggested they go together by train to Mongolia, crawling across Siberia in the process. She refused at first, but later got excited at the prospect of reading the petroglyphs found near Ulan Bator by Ramstedt and described by Pälsi.

Then everything went awry.

A cool, late afternoon light pressed against the snowy streets and the gates of the low houses built in the reign of Catharine the Great. There was a carefully stacked pile of firewood in the courtyard of a lovely old house. The fence around the hotel leaned steeply, the windows were filled with ice flowers. She was sitting in the lobby with its sumptuous bouquet of paper flowers. The atmosphere was Oblomovian, the snow of winter still falling. To the right of the reception desk was a hand-coloured photograph bordered in mourning of a sturdy woman wearing two medals on her chest.

The girl waited at least an hour before the young receptionist came sailing out of the back room wearing a muskrat hat, her lips roughly painted red. An elegantly sour cloud of eau de cologne spread around her. She didn't look at the girl, just paced back and forth as if she were in a hurry. When the girl managed to hand her the hotel voucher the receptionist went into the back room again and stayed there for another hour or two.

Her room was on the third floor. The hallway was stuffed with broken furniture and wooden crates, a beautiful redwood sofa sitting among the junk. On the wall was a print of Repin's Volga boatmen. An old floor monitor sat at a small table asleep.

The room was hot and cramped. The girl opened the small ventilation window. A spring wind came whirling into the room, grabbed hold of the light yellow curtains and fanned them. The window opened out onto an adjoining park.

There were pure white starched sheets on the bed, and bedbug spray in a corner of the bathroom. She got undressed and slid into the clean bed. She watched the little plastic satellite swinging between the curtains and fell asleep to the heavy hum of the gas boiler.

When she woke up she moved the bed in front of the window, pushed the curtains out of the way, and lay down. In the centre of the park below was a path surfaced in red sand. Farther off was a little frozen pool, its surface bright and smooth. There was no snow on top of the ice – the winds of April had blown it away. A bronze fish swam stiffly in the middle of the pool; perhaps, in the summer, water sprayed from its mouth. Waxwings twittered shrilly in the branches of the maple trees, waved their yellow-tipped tails, flicked their crests, and flew off now and then to follow the trolleybuses and trams into town. They flew up to the sky and watched the life of the city from there, then returned to the maple branches and the back of the rain-spattered park bench.

After noon, a loudspeaker wired to the gatepost of the park started playing Claude Debussy's *Prélude à l'après-midi d'un faun*. Soon old men started to arrive at the park to click dominoes. Then the old women appeared. Each of them put her own cloth on a bench and sat down.

The girl ate lunch in the hotel dining room: borscht, smetana and black bread. She looked at the hundred-light chandelier that hung from the dining-room ceiling, defying all artistic conventions. The waiter, who had a large mouth and small eyes, asked her if she'd like to exchange any money or sell any Western goods.

After lunch she walked through the mild weather to Victory Park and was startled by the metal clang of the tram wobbling past beyond the hedgerow. A black rat appeared beside her. It was sick, and thus not afraid of people. When she stopped, the rat stopped. She felt lonely.

She thought about Irina's earrings, her tailored skirt, her eyes, with a gaze you couldn't be sure of. It had been easy to be with Irina. Even the silence had a lightness. Irina accepted her and allowed her into her family, and when Mitka was shut up in the hospital, she and Irina had spent a lot of time together.

Irina had taken her to the monastery town of Zagorsk, whose church clock's insane, fifteen-tone jangle had rung in her head for a week after their visit; to Pasternak's dacha in Predelkino with its garden full of crushed eggshells painted different colours; to Konstantin Simonov's veranda, to Arseni Tarkovsky's grave, where they ate pumpkin seeds; and to the Vaganskoya Cemetery to look at the mound covered in flowers at Vladimir Vysotsky's grave. Irina read aloud to her from Marina Tsvetaeva and Osip Mandelstam's poems and encouraged her to read Turgenev, Lermontov, Bunin, Leskov, Platonov, Ilf and Petrov, and Trifonov.

They got to know each other better and gradually fell in love.

The girl bent down to look at the rat. It was dead. Its soul had abandoned its sick body. She sensed that Irina was think-ing about her.

She turned onto a path that took her to a black grove filled with chill mist. Hidden within it was a statue of Pushkin covered in something that looked like seaweed; a handful of rifle shell casings lay among the shards of broken vodka bottles that covered the ground beneath it.

She wandered into an open part of the park where the mist had faded and the air was translucent. Rachmaninov piano music played and the old men clicked their dominoes and the old ladies whispered among themselves on the benches. A light thaw slipped into the park and grew gradually into a warm spring day. An east wind blew the clouds hurriedly west. Somewhere in the distance roosters who'd lost their sense of time crowed. The snow that was everywhere melted into little streams. The girl found an empty bench. She fell asleep in the heat of the sunlight and started awake when a tremendous rushing sound invaded deep into her sleep. A surge of brown water was coming towards her from the other side of the park. The old men and women were gone, but the piano music was still playing. A lame horse was approaching along the path. It stopped when she dashed past it.

She ran to the hotel and straight to the third floor. She looked out of her window and saw water rising at tremendous speed, quickly covering half the park.

She ran back down to the lobby and rapped loudly on the reception desk. The receptionist with the fur hat emerged from the distant back room. The girl asked why so much water was suddenly rising. The clerk explained that the temperature had risen quickly overnight and the ice on the Angara had broken free. She said it was all perfectly normal and that it would recede by the next morning, or the next week, unless it rose higher.

The girl stood there astonished and at the same time relieved. She heard the receptionist talking to someone in the back room.

'Pavel Ivanovich. The one who's the district inspector for cultural affairs.'

'Forty-something? Kind of a wreck?'

'That's the one.'

'The fellow who likes to have three spoons of dill water every day before breakfast?'

'That's him. He told Zoya, and Zoya told me ...'

In the afternoon the water had disappeared from the park completely and taken all the snow with it, leaving no trace but the dirty ice and steaming, muddy ground.

It was evening. A carmine red tram cut along the edge of the boulevard. The black trees in the park stared at her gloomily, but she paid no attention to them. She was looking higher up, at the stars as they rattled like ice cubes in a green sky, and at the moon radiating its frozen light. The tall buildings nestled in the cold, gleaming along either side of the icy road. The street lights came on with a quiet hiss. They spilled a rattling bluish light for a long time, until the colour turned purplish red.

She turned on a black-and-white television that stood on a table in a corner of the room. It was showing an ad for the Soviet Union.

She thought about Mitka and felt sorry for him. But what if

the Crimean rest and treatment healed him? What would she do then? What about Irina? The whole thing worried her so that she started to soothe herself with memories: the times she and Mitka had listened to records on the cute little poison-green record player, sipped tea and champagne, played various board games thousands of times, laughed, rolling and shrieking with delight. They had known how to enjoy life, but then the evening turned to night, summer to autumn, and Mitka had to go to the loony bin.

From the big window in the lobby you could see the eaves, icicles hanging from them like a row of swords ready to slice in two the head of any random passer-by. A longhaired black cat slept on top of a lamppost that spewed bright yellow light. When she told the receptionist that she was going to continue her journey the woman asked her to wait a moment and went into the back room. When she returned she had a cream-coloured plastic model of the Kremlin tower in her hand.

'This is for you, Miss. A little memento of Irkutsk.'

When she stepped into the compartment the man was sitting on his bunk wearing long army underwear, filing his toenails.

She handed him the stack of newspapers she'd bought, which smelled of petrol. He said the train wasn't leaving until morning. She wasn't alarmed at this news.

She sat on her bunk for a long time and smiled. She watched him. He had a tired, cloudy look in his eyes, but that felt homely to her.

Clouds sailed across the darkening sky, colliding with each other. Eventually the night poured heavy and peaceful over the train.

The weightless, quiet morning light of early spring awoke her long before the station bell rang for the third time, the engine gave a heavy sigh, and the train rocked into motion.

IRKUTSK IS LEFT BEHIND; a silent, icebound, springtime city. Irkutsk, the yellow tiles of the university library, the pink onion church, the parks and trees, the noisy, steamy communal saunas, the tired land, the park covered in rusty floodwaters, the classical music in the little loudspeaker at the gate of the park, the soft drifts of snow in courtyard gardens. Irkutsk is left behind as an approaching electric train sways on the next track, house after small, sturdy little house, the white window frames, the flowery shutters, the eaves with their whimsical carvings, the lonely nineteen-storey prefab buildings in the middle of fields, the early spring sunshine, the smoking chimneys, the man standing atop a woodpile – this is still Irkutsk – the Russian-blue station building and the jungly, impenetrable forest. The bogs, the stunted trees, the waste, the logging lines – this is no longer Irkutsk. BAM railway tracks swallowed by the swamp, a house collapsed under snow. A few bittersweet accordion notes with accompanying bells drift through the next compartment. The train plunges into nature, throbs across the snowy empty land. Everything is in motion: snow, water, air, trees, clouds, wind, cities, villages, people, thoughts.

The train glided slowly along the lovely rough banks of Lake Baikal, across sudden cuts in the rock, through dozens of tunnels. An island with a bowed back rose up almost touching the shore, its lone tree a pine snag, a sea eagle in its crown watching the moving train. Baikal was as large as the sea, as broad as outer space. The girl imagined the ultramarine water full of hidden rocks, reefs, great islands, sunken vessels, drowned sailors, the bodies of extinct animals. Maybe fish. The ice had already shifted enough that broad cracks had appeared on the surface. She didn't see any Baikal seals. A sobbing wind blew from the north and stirred the dark water between the sheets of ice. Gnarled, melted old birches grew in every direction and covered the western sky with their branches. Round mounds of ice rose into the air around inlets sheltered by sparse beds of reeds. On one shore was an enormous factory complex, its thick chimneys pushing red clouds into the air. The name of the factory was written in letters the size of trucks on a boulder between two factory buildings: Voroshilov. She thought about Moscow, its cloudy November days, its cold March nights, the Moscow River whose shores she'd walked many times, its frothing waters and fish rotting among the rocks along the banks.

The man opened a bottle of vodka and poured two glasses.

'Do you know what happened to Gagarin when he was orbiting the earth in his capsule? He realised that the earth is a little piece of shit in a great big universe and it could be destroyed at any moment. When he came back from space, he started drinking, even though he had access to every privilege: the cosmonauts' base grocery, the party bosses' sanatoriums, hospitals, Western medicines. Khrushchev even bought him a small plane to cheer him up! But then what happened? Gagarin flew up over the clouds searching for death. He didn't have to look long – he ran into a mountain and died. A toast to Yuri Gagarin, and to Belka and Strelka, the valiant cosmonaut dogs.'

On the northwest shore of the lake, almost touching the water, there was an onion-domed church that looked like a playhouse. Around the church were several arolla pines. Their limbs were swaying, dripping with sun-melted snow. A wind came up and the long, soft needles of the trees scratched at the tattered church walls. The girl imagined wild, restless stars peeking between the dense pine branches like fireflies once the heavy night descended. Two motorcycles with sidecars were crossing the ice. One sidecar was red and full of live chickens tethered together, the other was painted bright blue. Ice fishers crouched here and there. The train curved closer to the shoreline, its wheels screeching. The girl saw a small carousel buried in snow and children's climbing bars. The train wound slowly on, then whistled happily and hurried forward into a tunnel cut into the mountain. A quiet dusk descended over everything. The train rattled ahead lazily, then stopped altogether.

It stood in the dark tunnel for a couple of hours. The glaring rays of the compartment ceiling light etched into the vinyl floor. The girl could feel the man's breathing, the calm beating of his heart. He looked at her through heavy-lidded eyes.

'Here's a case from real life, my little berry,' he said, lounging back on his bunk. 'There was a fellow named Kolya who kicked it two days before he turned forty. We buried him in the new Moscow cemetery, right next to a beautiful girl named Anna Pavlovna Dorenko, who died young. A year passed and Ascension Day came. A magnetic wind was blowing from the north when I, Vova and Gafur decided to go say hello to our old friend at the cemetery. We took along a couple of bags of food and five bottles of vodka. Vova spread a tablecloth over the grave and Gafur put the food on it. We were offering Kolya some vodka and scattering a few Belomorkanal cigarettes on the grave when along came a sweet gaggle of girls and before the night was half over I was screwing one of those hefty little chickens. This chick was lying on top of the grave with her drumsticks spread and I was staring at Anna Pavlovna's pretty face painted on the headstone. Anna was looking back at me, smiling. For the first time in my life I thought that there might be something after death.'

The girl opened the compartment door a crack. A little girl with braided pigtails was playing in the corridor with a matryoshka doll. Soon the littlest doll, the one the carver hadn't bothered to carve completely and the painter hadn't painted properly, fell out of her hands and rolled down the corridor carpet towards the WC, whose door was open.

The man sat on his bunk in a colourful shirt and looked tiredly out the window. There was nothing to see but the stone wall of the tunnel, with the words *Baikal is being destroyed* painted on it in red letters.

'Do you know what a Viennese quadrille is? It goes like this. They take fifty men out of a dungeon and they truck them to the place of execution. When they get there, they order them to line up. They let them count off, maybe by eights. In other words, every eighth man is shot, and the rest are trucked back to the dungeon to wait another night. But but but … the quadrille is the part before every eighth man is shot, when they make them all change places in line six times or more. First you're third, then you're fifth, then you're first, and on it goes.'

The train eased forward and out of the tunnel. The brightness of the spring day stabbed their eyes. Someone cheered. The shores of Baikal spread on either side.

'Last year at this same time I was looking out of this same window watching a rescue helicopter trying to pick up some frozen fishermen from a drifting piece of ice. It's the same thing every spring. The fishermen sit on the ice, the ice starts to move, and they're left drifting on a raft. Some of them drown, some freeze to death, some are rescued. Why in the world do they rescue them? Nobody makes them go out there.'

The rails curved gradually landward. Low dark clouds started to move in from the east. Along the edge of a rolling field abutting the tracks an old willow grouse flapped its wings. Farther away lay a low tumbledown greenhouse with a *kolkhoz* barn beyond it. In front of the barn was a horse and a load of hay. Two women were busy on top of the hay, one young and one old. They were shoving tufts of hay through the loft window into the barn. A black blanket was folded over the horse's back and it was chomping the hay, calm and hearty. A sooty old kick sled poked out of a heap of snow. The girl could hear someone walking past the open compartment door saying that Lake Baikal cleans itself.

'The Tatars have a custom of tying prisoners of war to dead soldiers,' the man said. 'Leg to leg, belly to belly, face to face. That way the dead kill the living. You can achieve some things with good, but all things with evil. There's no point fighting evil. You can't get rid of it, no matter how much you talk about some god's goodness.'

The rails groaned through the green darkness. Lake Baikal was left far behind. The girl imagined the strange fishes that dwelt in its secret depths, the flocks of jellyfish floating like clouds deep under the water.

Suddenly the engine braked angrily. The train was

approaching a station, stirring up a wind that grabbed the granular snow that had fallen overnight, tossing it in every direction. They stopped at Ulan Ude station.

She stepped lazily off the train onto the platform. Three cats were walking towards her. One had a broken tail, the second was sleek, with a curious smile, and the third had had its ears cut off, and staggered over the clean-swept platform like a drunk.

A raw northeast wind came carrying sharp balalaika notes. Silent, exhausted engines lay on the tracks. The man ran past wearing only his inside shirt, past the street sweeper, towards the station building. The milk-white, fast-falling sky started to throw cold, drizzling sleet on the wind-beaten ground. All of space was filled with a depressing bleakness.

When the man came back he had a jar of smetana and a shopping bag in one hand and a bouquet of chrysanthemums wrapped in a *Pravda* in the other. He handed her the flowers, winked, and bustled into the train. He had a bottle of vodka under each arm. A local commuter train twitched and buzzed as it moved to the neighbouring track. The crowd emerging from it puffed out a cloud of mingled smells of home. The wind grabbed the cloud and slammed it into her. She got on the train and went to her compartment. The man sat on his bunk with a serene expression and put the bottles down in the middle of the table.

'Here's two bottles full of a booze they call vodka. My kind of country. Even though there's prohibition, they have their own provincial worries here in this valley. You can't order people around in the borderlands.'

He shifted his gentle gaze to her.

'Did you know, Baba Yaga, that we are now in the capital of the Buryat Autonomous Soviet Socialist Republic? They have a strange, slurring language here and worship Buddha and Jesus at the same time.'

He pointed at her hair.

'A fringe in front and undone at the back. Not terribly stylish.' He laughed, laid a fatherly hand over her hand, and gave it a squeeze.

'We suit each other. The witch and Koschei the Deathless, the devil soul … There are more than a hundred ethnic groups in this country. If one of them, or two or three, are destroyed, it's a small matter. They herd reindeer in the north and make wine in Georgia. Here we have the northern tundra and endless forests. In the south are the steppes, in the southeast are deserts of sand, and in the Caucasus the mighty mountains, with the pass crawling between them. The wind sighs over the pass and carries big clouds with it. There are the beaches of the Crimea and the swamps of Belarus. There's dancing the trepak in birchbark shoes along the Volga, screaming Chechen circle games, the Yakuts' shaman drums, the Chukchis, the Ainus, the Samoyeds, the Koryaks with their reindeer, the Kalmuks with their sheep and the Cossacks with their sables, Tambovian ham, Volgan sterlet, Razan apples. What else … never mind. A Georgian once told me that the history of the Georgians and Armenians was longer and more beautiful than the Russians'. He said the Georgians were building churches and composing poetry when the Russians were still grunting and living in caves. That's a lie.'

The train gave a hoarse whistle and its wheels lurched into motion with a whoop. Arisa stood on the top step of the carriage holding the door frame with one hand and swinging a foot in the air.

'All the far-flung peoples and their fine culture are blossoming like they never have before, although they ought to become Russians. All of these thousands of languages that are kept alive year after year when the Russian language would suffice. We Russians are an undemanding, resilient, patient bunch. We grant some space to others. But it can't go on like this forever.'

He took a needle and thread out of his bag and started to repair the bag handle. Between stitches he glanced at the loudspeaker, which was playing Beethoven's Seventh.

'If it just had a little singing with it. That damned roaring grows hair in your ears.'

The sizeable city of Ulan Ude, with the world's largest head of Lenin in its central square, disappeared in the distance. The train rattled through snow-capped mountains and wild wastes of taiga buried in snow. Rows of black hills spread at the edge of the flat landscape. She thought about Mitka and the chicken wire in the corridor window at the mental hospital. According to the military doctor's diagnosis, Mitka was psychotic and was given antipsychotic medication. When a healthy person is forced to take that kind of medicine it can't be good for them. Mitka got really sick in the hospital, wasn't able to eat, his mental state pathetic.

A spoon tinkled in a tea glass. The man fussed with his vodka bottles between bouts of sewing, wiping them and examining the labels and checking to see if the corks were firmly in place. But he didn't open them. He just looked and admired.

'Fellows like me, when we have to choose between two evils, we always take both.'

A little later he spread some celery stalks and garlic chives on the table and opened a jar of cold borscht. He handed the girl a gigantic spoon. He smacked his lips and sniffed, his big ears wiggling. At regular intervals he added a splash of boiling water and smetana to the soup. It tasted good. The scent of the celery stalks filled the compartment. He handed her a Pepsi.

'Seems to me you ought to have at least one taste of home on this trip, my girl. This is Brezhnev's drink. That's why I don't drink it.'

The train arrived in Khabarovsk station in the middle of the night. The station sign was covered in a thick layer of snow, as were the tops of the railway carriages sleeping along the tracks. She hurried off the train. A burning night frost seized her face. The air was so brittle it was difficult to breathe. A few street lamps oozed the faintest yellowish light as they struggled to illuminate the station. The city was so full of thick night that she almost turned back.

She pushed herself forward and walked with squeaking steps into the station. There were no people there. The ticket windows were closed and the trinket kiosks sulked empty in the darkness.

She walked across the station hall, past a kiosk that sold plastic pens and journals. A fat cat came to meet her. It looked at her with curiosity, waved its tail, leapt over a mound of snow carried in on travellers' shoes, and disappeared behind a newspaper stand. In front of the main doors was a large puddle from earlier in the day chilled by the night, a skiff of ice gleaming on its surface.

Along the edge of the railway square were two black Volgas with feminine smiles and elk-hood ornaments, one Moskvich, a little red Yalta, and a poison-green Pobeda. The engines were running, the drivers chatting in a circle. The square was filled with dense exhaust. She approached the men warily and asked if any of them could drive her to the Hotel Progress. The men erupted in laughter. A black-whiskered man with a flashing gold tooth grabbed her knapsack and directed her to the Moskvich.

He turned on the radio and for a moment Galina Vishnevskaya filled the car with Tatiana's letter aria. The gearbox complained and the engine roared, drowning out the aria. Spring slush frozen by nighttime cold shone in the light of a half moon. The driver turned to look at her.

'Khabarovsk is the world's most beautiful border city. We have the greatest wonder of the twentieth century, the Khabarovsk Bridge. On the other side is China, which is a province of ours. If you like I can show you the bridge tomorrow. I can meet you in front of the hotel at noon. All right?'

The taxi's green light flashed and the car disappeared into the impenetrable mist. She breathed in the big city night. It smelled familiar, like old charred iron and oven-fresh steel. The sky over the city was pitch black to the south, but in the east the dirty lights of the distant harbour blinked, and in the sky one red star twinkled.

She pounded for a long time on the door of the sixteen-storey hotel before a sleepy, grey-haired woman came with slippers on her feet to open it. The hotel lobby was very dimly lit. On the walls were side-by-side copies of Cezanne's fruit and Vasnetsov's warriors. She handed the woman her hotel voucher, filled out the stack of grubby forms, and climbed thirteen flights to her room because the lift wasn't working.

The room was large and the bed was broad and clean. The radiator hissed like a steam iron. She turned on the tap in the bathtub. It angrily spat brown water. The city was deep in sleep.

The misty gloom of a frosty morning covered half of the yellow moon, a quick purple flashing in the eastern sky. From between her rustling sheets, she looked at the polyester, tobacco-smoke-scented shade of the reading lamp. She'd seen the same kind of lamp before but she couldn't remember where. She pulled aside the stained curtains and let the morning in.

The sun hung over the opposite shore of the Amur River, in China. It poured its frozen rays towards the flat roofs of the highrises. In the middle of the river a shipping channel flowed; loose rafts of ice had been squeezed to pack ice during the night. A carmine red tram rattled far below with a loud clang.

The living sun started to move. It crawled from the open ice of the Amur and over the snowy rooftops of the awakening city. Tawny light, a funnelled current of small snowflakes, and the bustle of city-dwellers rushing to work drifted through the open vent window into the room. Unhurried people the size of ants half hidden by banks of snow strolled along the treeless boulevard with grocery bags, boxes of smoked fish, and jars of pickles. A chimney-sweep busied himself with an ancient piece of cable in the chimney of a green block of flats. A lustre of frost sparkled on the car roofs, horns grunted, engines whined, exhaust pipes scraped against the frozen asphalt, trolleybuses sparked, trams clunked from stop to stop.

She took a shower, dried her hair, dressed herself lazily, with voluptuous slowness, and went down to the hotel restaurant, where she was served lukewarm tea and good fatty fish.

The beaten-up, seemingly hand-built Moskvich was sputtering outside, waiting for her. The driver nodded complacently when he saw her. She stood in front of the hotel for a moment and listened to the poignant song of an accordion drifting from a distant street, a tune about love that's never requited, and slid into the back seat. The Moskvich shot out into the snowy street with a cough. The sooty crud from the nearby factories emerged from beneath the pure, sun-melted snow.

The driver watched her in the rearview mirror. He was a weatherbeaten old man with a back bent by heavy labour, a creased face, and faded eyes. His thick eyebrows grew together and his sideburns met his beard. He had dressed his sparse hair with home brew and combed it neatly. He had looked quite different the night before. She didn't even see a gold tooth now.

'Are you a surveyor?' he asked.

She didn't say anything. He glanced at her in the mirror again.

'A geologist, then? A foreign geologist from Moscow? I'll drive you wherever you like, but first the news from Moscow, eh? How's Red Square? Same as always? And the Moscow River? How many cars are there in Moscow?'

The Moskvich raced skidding past a dried-up, five-cornered

fountain that a group of Chinese tourists was photograph-ing. The sun-warmed crusty snow floated across the rooftops and fell crashing in great sheets onto the pavements. Beautiful Siberian people, strong and handsome, formed twisted queues in front of the food shops. The spring wind howled where the roads intersected.

The driver turned into a roundabout. On the right was a heap of bright watermelons, defying the slippery spring ground. On the left was a jumble of discarded wooden crates that looked like Mayakovsky's staircase.

He dropped her off next to the bridge.

In spite of the bright sunlight, the bridge was lit with floodlights at the edge of the water, their unreal illumination causing a strange distortion in perspective. It was as if the bridge wriggled over the water. She looked over the bridge at the trucks crossing and the silhouettes of the buildings in the harbour. She stood in front of the bridge beams, far from the border guards' booths.

A pallid blue sky shimmered over the river. The April morning wind whistled past and struck her face with a handful of grainy snow. She leaned against a beam and looked down at the river. Slush churned like something alive in the lead-grey water of the shipping channel and along the shore. A bright blue oil drum floated among it. The channel was crowded. Two Chinese icebreakers ploughed through the pack ice. Chinese, Korean and Russian cargo ships with their horns blaring, long barges, tugboats, dredgers, and ferries of various sizes slid through the icy slush. Brown splashes of water rose over the ice along the shore.

She walked to a bus stop. The snow smelled like spring. A

woman walked past dolled up, her flowered skirt fluttering in the breeze. She was holding a small heron with stained feathers and one wing hanging limp.

The girl got on the bus, sat down behind the hiccuping driver and rode to Okhotsk, the city's largest harbour.

She got off and walked along the shore, which was in places a mixture of ice and slushy mud. She spent a long time looking at a wrecked ship, rusted through, lying on its side, listened to the melancholy howl of the wind and the noisy clank of the harbour machinery. She soon came to a place where the waves on the shore were churning wildly, carrying off great blocks of ice and crashing them against the steep rocks. The surface of the water was rising visibly, and the ice with it. Two men were crouched on the shelf of rock, their small Yalta parked on the sand farther away. They had a campfire on the rocks, too, where they were roasting fish on sticks.

They gestured for her to come over. The winter sun had toasted both their faces brown and the fronts of their coats were covered in fish scales. One of them smelled of resin, the other of fortified wine. Both smelled of squalor.

'A magnetic storm's about to come up and take the ice with it. You shouldn't be walking on the shore.'

They offered her some foul-smelling vodka and nice-tasting fish. The man who smelled of resin, who had unbelievably bad teeth, told her that the previous summer a toxic spill from China had killed almost all the fish.

'We used to get pike, catfish, carp and ruffe out of this river. Now nothing. I keep fishing, because I always have. You can't change a man's nature.'

Disregarding his warnings, she continued strolling down

the shore past a rusted boiler, old locks, an enormous buoy, a bicycle gear, a copper cylinder, a small motor, plugs, corks, broken vodka bottles, metal buckets with no bottoms, an oily enamel pot, plum weights, water pipes, steel pellets, a steering wheel from a tractor, bedsprings, and a metal sign rusted through that read TECHNOLOGICAL-SCIENTIFIC ORGANISATION OF INDUSTRIAL POWER ENGINE VIBRATOR RESEARCH. The lively early spring sunshine melted the ice from the shore. The wind sighed and the river smelled of rot. The odour of decayed wood, sodden sawdust, household trash, oil, naphtha, and the foamy residue left by the barges covered over the ineffable scent of the ice breaking up.

In shady spots there was still some pure, powdery spring snow, where marsh birds were happily pecking at holes in the river ice with their slippery beaks. Someone had painted in white on one of the rocks: *Down with Yermak, Down with Stalin-Hitlers.* The mysterious wind tore at the sides of a small barge caught among the pack ice, and a thin puff of blue smoke rose from the battered chimneys of the spruce-walled harbour buildings.

She climbed up the bank. A vast flock of a thousand wild geese was gliding just over her head. The muddy masses of water flowing from farther upstream lifted the rafts of ice higher and higher. The rumbling grew louder. Then the last of the surface ice crumbled into great chunks that hurled themselves over each other and climbed crashing up the shore. Nothing could stop the power of the ice. It could crush the shore, the docks, the buildings. She climbed up onto a boulder. There was a heart carved into it with 'Valentina + Volodya 14.8.1937' written inside.

She climbed higher and saw a little park a short distance away. There was a trodden path leading to it. She went and sat down to rest for a moment on a bench. The tranquil clouds looking down from the pale sky smelled like spring. She listened to the sound of the far-off Okhotsk Sea and looked at the half-built modern blocks of flats that seemed to press themselves quietly into the earth. A military band appeared from behind an arolla pine. They advanced towards the park's small fountain with stiff steps, wearing black cloaks and billed hats of black fur. There was a post in front of the snow-filled fountain with a tin-shaded lamp on top that rattled loudly in the river breeze. The band tuned their wind-chilled instruments, the conductor's baton fluttered, and a light military march rang in the air.

As evening fell, needles of ice began to fall. She wandered some more in the city. The glaring red, dying sunlight lingered over the bumpy streets. As she walked farther from the city centre the streets became narrower and more rundown, meandering capriciously, then turning straight and clear. She missed Moscow and the Arbat, where the narrow streets zigzagged delightfully. The fitful east wind started to turn into a snowstorm. It ripped at the clouds and cleared the sky. She headed back to the middle of town.

She went straight to the hotel restaurant. There were three signs on the restaurant door: CLOSED, CLOSED FOR DINNER, CLOSED FOR INVENTORY. The restaurant was full. She stepped inside. In addition to local diners there were a few Chinese salesmen, a couple of Koreans, and a few Japanese hotel guests sitting in the dining room. A pear-shaped waitress showed her to a table by the window where a thin woman with a shaggy fur hat and a lively face was sitting. The two of them looked sometimes at the other diners, sometimes at each other. The woman took a pretty packet of cigarettes out of her Yugoslavian purse and smoked one in a yellow amber cigarette holder. Her wrists were delicate and graceful.

The girl ordered millet porridge, sauerkraut and cutlets, peas steeped in vodka, leeks, and scrambled eggs with sliced tomatoes.

'Is everything all right in your bathroom?' the woman asked. 'I can't sleep because the gas boiler clanks and whistles all night. I'm not used to that kind of noise. I've been on the taiga for fifteen months and this city life gets on my nerves.'

She smiled, straightened her hat, and took out another cigarette. 'We've been looking for oil for months in the far north. We didn't find any this time.'

She lit the cigarette and looked at its glowing tip for a long time. 'If we do find oil, they'll bulldoze the village and put an oil rig in its place. Shoot the dogs, since they won't be needed any more. The people in the village will be shipped somewhere else – the next village, which could be three hundred kilometres away. There are no roads, of course.'

She blew smoke gently towards the single pink carnation sitting primly in its long-necked vase.

'This time we ended up having to leave empty-handed. All that's left is a village ravaged by jeeps, tractors and earthmovers. That's their gain, our loss. Now I'm flying to Moscow to rest. I have three months' holiday. I'll go walking down Mira Prospekt with my deadbeat friends and sit in cafés talking clever nonsense. After three months off, I'll be perfectly glad to come back here. I like it here. Don't you?'

She looked at the girl and tilted her head slightly. 'I'm not married, because I like being around people. I think like Chekhov: if you love solitude, get married.'

There were at least ten waitresses at the counter. At one end sat a bloated cashier; the young men waiting to unload their trucks were making her laugh with their talk. A stiff-backed doorman was chatting with the old woman supervisor. She sat erect behind her little table, wrapped in a shawl knitted from thick angora, sharpening her pencil. On the table was a green plastic telephone and a brown calendar. Some aged cleaners sat in a corner of the entryway with tin buckets at their feet and enormous black rags in their hands. The bussers had taken over one table, the coat check had fallen asleep in his squeaky chair among the heavy winter coats.

An orchestra dressed in matching dark suits appeared on the restaurant stage. The bassist was Chinese; the drummer looked Korean. The first notes of 'Moscow Lights' drifted over the tobacco-smoke-softened dance floor.

A fashionable young Japanese man asked the woman to dance. The pair moved slowly over the parquet floor, which was lit by a plastic crystal chandelier that reached in every direction. The joys and sorrows of the city, falling asleep in the night damp, condensed beneath it.

Outside, the snowflakes gathered in a freezing whirlwind; a statue of Lenin blithely waving his hand peered in at the restaurant window. The woman said her goodbyes and left with the Japanese man into the bowels of the hotel.

The girl left the restaurant. The cloudless, starless, faded sky kept her company in the quiet, dream-sunken city. She peeped into a beer house on a side street. A puff of sour tobacco smoke blew over her face. She hesitated a moment, then went in, curious. Two peasants lay passed out on the slushy floor. She ordered a mug of beer, but got a purplish, bad-tasting ale. She put the mug down and left.

The dense, deserted night gathered around her. The city was inhabited only by the night wind, a hiss of snow. She passed the statue of Khabarov holding a miserable spruce sapling, walked along a boulevard lined with deciduous trees, and looked at the marvellous ornamental carvings on the stone houses. At every crossroads, she chose the smaller street. The houses were dark, with a faint yellow light glowing in just a few of the windows.

Irina had kissed her for the first time in the Lenin Mausoleum. It had happened so quickly and gently that the young soldiers on guard didn't notice. Or if they did, they didn't believe their eyes. When they got back home, Mitka greeted her and his mother with a crooked smile on his face. She had to wait a long time for the second kiss, but once it happened, there was no turning back. It happened at the same time that Mitka was lying in restraints in a lunatic asylum. And then the day came when Mitka was set free. It was a day of great happiness, but she and Irina knew that the worst was yet to come for the three of them.

After she'd walked far enough to the south and to the north, she decided to take the tram back to the hotel.

There was a large department store in the middle of the town. A dirty yellow pile of snow loomed next to it, and in front of the entrance spread a puddle of mud the size of a small pond that the customers carefully skirted. A stately gull stood in the middle of the puddle. She climbed to the top of the high, slippery staircase and bought a little bottle of Red Moscow perfume and two chocolate bars. One had a picture of Pushkin on the label, the other a smiling little girl in a babushka. As she finally walked to the station with hurried steps, a wild red star fell behind a rose bush covered in evening frost, the street lights silently went out, and she was surrounded by a growing Asian darkness. She could hear the far-off whistle of the train and see the tracks gleaming in the dusk. A local train crawled up beside her and a flood of workers emerged from within, brushing past her on both sides.

She hurried in the cold to the half-opened door and into the station. The oily floor shone. Drops of light from the crystal chandeliers twinkled in the puddles on the floor. There, under the arched ceiling of the station, she met the man. He smelled of sauerkraut, vodka, onion soup, and the pharmacy. His presence calmed her fearful mood.

'You've probably noticed by now that all the cities and villages are alike. If you've seen one, you've seen them all. But let's go get a bite of vermicelli and chicken broth. We'll be on our way to the land of the Mongols soon.'

THE TALL, THICKSET HEAD CONDUCTOR put a whistle to his lips and blew long on it. The engine howled three times and the train slammed into motion. The engine's wheels beat sparks from the rails and the rough cheer of Khachaturian's 'Sabre Dance' rang out of the beige plastic loudspeaker.

The man scowled at the speaker's broken volume knob, an unlit cigarette between his lips.

'A flock of geese born out of somebody's arse,' he said, grabbing his pillow and pressing it hard against the speaker. 'I don't enjoy killing a sensitive piece of music, but I have no choice.'

Khabarovsk is left behind, the smoke from the windowless factories and the clouds of spring-melted toxins. Khabarovsk is left behind, the Paris of Siberia, the stone buildings with their ornaments covered in a patina of time. A land killed by oil and heavy industry and discarded, a heavy city surrounded by crumbling slabs of steel-reinforced concrete, where women walk the back streets in high-heeled fur boots, left behind. The decomposing municipal combine built of Chinese steel, the reeking fish cannery, left behind. Khabarovsk, the dimly lit, beautiful city, the tired land, left behind. This is still Khabarovsk: an abandoned industrial strip, a planted pine forest, a stillborn, half-built suburb, the polluted sick forest, the dense larch forest, a woman with a sack of food, the crudely retouched photos of the General Secretaries on the telephone poles. The train picks up speed. The fifth cluster of prefab buildings, which they call suburbs, the little houses defeated in the battle of life, the open land, the Chinese forest, the fallow earth, the lonely nineteen-storey building in the middle of the fields. The last remains of a factory rush past in the distance with the speed of the train, then deep forest, wetland, spruce trees, the mountains of Japan beyond the horizon, sake and haikus. This is no longer Khabarovsk. The train moves on. A collapsed house under snow, a village of two dozen houses among the geriatric underbrush, a glitter of golden lights from a quarry. The train plunges into nature, throbs across the snowy, empty land. Everything is in motion: snow, water, air, trees, clouds, wind, cities, villages, people, thoughts.

The music gradually went quiet and faded away. The man went to smoke his cigarette in the cold carriage entryway. He took heavy drags, smoking it down to his fingernails. A dense snowstorm whirled over the treeless steppe. In the middle of the plain of snow was a lightless, forgotten village. A lone crow fought against the wind atop a chimney gone cold. The man spread the draughts board on the table. They played silently. He won.

After the third game he snorted, 'There's no more stupid game than this, but still ...'

They played six more long games, so long that they both were spent. The man went to sleep. The girl missed Moscow. She thought about her last trip, when she and Mitka went to Kiev, sharing a compartment with two young men. One spent the whole trip moping, in his own world. The other was studying to be a machine draughtsman at the design institute, adored anything to do with numbers, charts, columns, sketches, specifications and, above all, coupons. He was flipping through them for the whole trip.

When Irina was seventeen and was pregnant with Mitka, Zahar had sent her to the Caucasus, to her aunt's house in the Lermontov mountains. While she was there she had fallen in love with a girl like herself, a student named Galina, and brought her home to Moscow. Galina, Irina, Mitka and Zahar had lived together in the same household with some other relatives for seven years. Then Galina moved away. According to Mitka, after that Irina had been with Tonya, Katya, Klasa and Julia, and perhaps others. When she and Mitka met, Julia was spending her nights in Irina's bedroom, but lived somewhere else. It all happened in secret. The girl didn't talk with Julia very much, although she saw her many times at the door to Irina's room or in the hallway. Mitka hated his mother's girl-friends. Not because they were women but because he wanted his mother all to himself – that's how he always put it.

Only two stars glimmered in the turquoise sky, very far apart. The heavy clouds nestled low, close to the ground. A cold, powerless desperation crept into her breast. She thought about how joys are forgotten but sorrow and stupidity never are.

A little yellow bird flew out of the bushes and up to the window. It looked in with disbelief, then flew away. An old electrician had climbed up a leaning telephone pole with a tangled coil of wire in one hand and a black receiver in the other. Beyond the electrician a swelling neon-yellow whirl of mist reared like a snake, wriggled upward with a hiss, and rose glittering towards the lid of sky. Then a second burning cloud of mist, and a third, and a fourth. The Northern Lights sparkled against the dome of clear blue sky, painting the snow green and the tail of a Siberian bluebill black. The taiga sucked the Northern Lights into itself and left the sky empty and clean. The taiga changed to a forest, the sea of forest to a sea of fields, the sea of fields to a sea of woodland wilderness. The man slept with an amusingly happy look on his face. She watched him for a long time, dozed off, woke for a moment, then drifted into a deep, deathlike sleep.

The man finished his morning exercises and poured a glass full of vodka. He handed the girl a glass of tea dregs.

'Let us wish for life and troubles, innocent laughter, crying for no reason, hearty merrymaking, mild hangovers, eternal health and a too-early death. Let's lift our glasses to the feminine beauty of our compartment and to the guardians of injustice, those sacks of garbage who couldn't get any other kind of work. And a toast to deception. May we be deceived in a better direction. Long live the militias.'

He tossed the whole contents down his throat in one motion, took a bite of raw onion, and filled his glass again.

'That's enough toasting and playing around, time to get drinking! A carriage of vodka, please.'

The glass emptied and was immediately filled again.

'Katyushka, my little silly head, couldn't stand fellows like me. That's why I fell in love with her. But I always say there's nothing in the world as fucked up as female logic.'

A thick snowstorm raged over the treeless steppe. The shy morning light tried to come out from between two grey clouds, unsuccessfully.

'Heart and logic. That's all there is ... I'm gonna have another drink or two, then we'll talk.'

He picked up his knife and scratched his elbow with it. His eyes were glistening as if he'd just been crying.

'So. Once on the Volga or the Yenisei, somewhere around there, a boy and his mother and father. The boy heard his father tell his mother she had to choose, the boy or him. To which she answered, Don't worry, he'll be dead soon, and we can be alone. The next morning the boy said goodbye to his three-legged dog and never came back. He joined others like himself and started living on the street, selling himself for bread. He whispered in the men's ears, I'm a little boy from Odessa ...'

After an hour he opened another bottle. Then he opened a third – his last one – and poured his glass full, but didn't drink it all, just rinsed his throat a little. He moved the empty bottle from the table to the floor.

'I won't waste compliments on you. I'm just going to say it outright, dear travelling companion. Would you give me some, just once? It's not as if it can wear out.'

A shy smile came over his face. The girl sat up on the edge of her bunk. The snowy ocean of forest spread shoreless, filling the whole landscape. Waves of forest receding to the horizon, dropping into valleys, curving over the flat sides of a hill. Between the slopes wound a little river. Thick red water flowed through its melted depths. The man tossed a haughty, sly look at her.

'Just let me ...'

She looked him straight in the eye. He dropped his gaze and looked at his hands, frozen in thought. The passionate sighs of the engine carried into the compartment.

'It was there that I fucked Vimma, and everything was right on track. That was my life. But then something came up that offered some money. It's easy to turn down groceries, but not money. Vimma and I had a difference of opinion and I stabbed her six times with a Siberian knife. I was trying to hit her heart, but evidently God was protecting her and she walked out of our apartment and into the neighbour's, and that was the last I ever saw of her. Years later I heard from a card shark that Vimma had been seen as a bride at the Karabash camp. She was celebrating a lesbian wedding, singing about how she never wanted to come back to civilian life.

'Don't believe everything I feed you, my girl.'

The man was suddenly quiet and stayed quiet for a long time, smacking his dry lips and sniffling.

'Russian whores don't understand anything. All you get from them is a rotting cock. The ruined beauty of old whores. It speaks to my dick.'

He grabbed the front of his pants. His face softened into open desire.

'Just one time. It would make life so much more bright and beautiful, honest it would. It always does.'

The sunset burned itself out. Evening had come.

'We could start a tab, the way Soviet whores do, or do your people pay with crisp new bills? Money's not good enough? No, it's not. Once the desire's gone, roubles can't help. You're from a rich country. You can wipe your cunt with my roubles.'

He stared at her, his head tilted slightly, like a scolded child.

'One hundred and twenty-five, your highness. Will that do it? I want to see what the difference is between a Finnish cunt and a Russian one. Or should I call it a pussy, since I'm in the presence of a lady?'

He was quiet for a moment, then squinted and groaned.

'I don't care if you've fucked a hundred hot Finnish boys

and sucked their dicks till your cheeks were hollow. I never turned something down because it was second-hand.'

He knelt on the floor and started kissing her knees. She pushed him away. He picked his knife up from the table.

'Any chick will do it if you give them a little tickle with a knife on the carotid artery. Unfortunately, I'm not that kind of man.'

He slipped the knife under his mattress. Then he got up and flopped right on top of her. He smelled of swamp mist and herring and his heart was beating heavy and fast. After a moment he burst into insane laughter. He coughed up so much drunken laughter in her face that her cheeks were hot.

'My little whore, I could stick this stump of cock through you like you were made of head cheese. But no. Listen to me – there isn't a torture invented that a Russian can't withstand. We can withstand anything. Including the fact that you can't always get some pussy when you want it.'

His sweaty, liquor-soaked words ran down the steamy walls of the compartment as he got up and sat on the edge of her bed.

'Now I need a glass of vodka to brighten my soul.'

He sloshed out a glassful, flicked some into his mouth, and looked like he was about to teeter over and lie down, but he got on his feet, swaying. The girl crouched in the doorway, ready to run into the corridor. He tumbled onto her bed again. He sat up with a groan, scratched at his chest hair, emptied his glass in two swallows, and looked at her wearily.

'Tomorrow, my little slut, I'm starting a new life. The denser the woods, the thicker the partisans.'

He let out a bloodless squeak, fell over again, buried his face in the pillow, bounced upright again, wrenched himself onto his feet, and staggered frighteningly to the middle of the floor. His gaze was dull and muddy, his lips wet with shouting.

'I envy the flies. Their lives are so easy.'

He hit the compartment door with his fist. It made his body rock. He started to cry, and in the middle of his cry broke out in a defiant laugh.

'Hit me. Hit me! Beat the old guy till he shits his pants. Give me one right in the mouth!'

He was yelling and sweat was running down his forehead. She sat where she was and didn't move. He fell on his knees, tried to touch her knees, and said in a soft voice, almost a whisper: 'At least hit me! Beat the shit out of an old goat, my little whore. My own little sadist. Kick me. Kick me in the kidneys so I can feel alive. Teach me about life and give me some peace. The rottenest Russian whore is better than you. I want to sleep and never wake up. Plug's pulled out, power's off … cut the cord.'

He staggered to the door and yelled down the hallway, 'Tea and a towel! Arisa! Tea and a towel!'

Sonechka soon appeared carrying a tray with two steaming glasses of tea and a clean hand towel. He quickly emptied both glasses. His face shone red and beads of sweat were running down his neck. He wiped away the sweat, wheezed once, and fell into a deep sleep. There were muffled voices in the next compartment.

The hot tea glasses had steamed up the window. Beyond it, snowy shadows of slender spruce trees kept watch over the dead taiga. Across a clearing in front of a clump of bushes stood an abandoned station. The train slid past it, causing such a burst of pressure that the frames around the broken windows fell out onto the frozen ground. Soon the spruces too were gone and a barren, almost desert landscape opened up around them.

The girl searched her bag for her drawing pad and found the gift that the hotel receptionist in Irkutsk had given her. She turned it over in her hands. It was a thermometer shaped like the Kremlin tower. She set it on the table next to the vase.

THE LIGHTS OF THE STATION gave a green tint to the snow and wind-torn newspaper. The girl heard Arisa shout, 'You can leave when you have permission! Until then everybody stay in your compartments!'

The train stood for a long time at the Naushki border station. The border militia gathered all the passengers' passports and carried the man away, limp. The customs officials started their ransacking ritual. The ceremony lasted six hours and ten minutes. They took her sketchbook when they left.

Just before the train gave a honk and started moving, the border guards dragged the man back into the compartment. He was snoring happily, drool running from between his grinding teeth out of the corner of his mouth and onto the pillow stained by his oily hair.

The train bleated, screeched, and leapt happily into motion. Tchaikovsky's Sixth Symphony flowed from the beige plastic speakers and over the passengers like a tank.

The girl got up, gathered the dirty tea glasses from the table, went into the corridor, and walked to the compartment of Arisa and Sonechka. Arisa asked her to sit down for a moment and enjoy a cup of lemon tea with them.

She nodded gratefully. She sat on the hard bed and looked at the bouquet of mustard-yellow chrysanthemums jutting out of a low vase. Arisa sliced the lemon with a dull knife and began to speak in an agitated voice.

'In January 1934 a railway official who was living in one of the cubicles in our commune died. The soup started boiling over before the body was even cold. My mother started a pitched battle over who would get the cubicle, and she wasn't averse to pulling hair to get it. The fight was settled one ordinary day when a woman moved into the cubicle. My mother called her Judas, although our neighbour Nyuta said that this ex-human had once been an important person, the secretary to some Trotskyite bureaucrat. I liked the woman. I asked if I could go to visit her while my mother was at work. My mother strictly forbade it and gave me a good whack on the ear to back up her words. The woman's name was Tamara Nikolayevna Berg. My father called her Mara, and he gave me permission to visit her when my mother wasn't home. We lived that way for a couple of years, and whenever my mother called her an expendable person and a Judas, my father shushed her. Then one day the woman was gone. The door to her cubicle was nailed shut. It wasn't until after my mother died that my father told me that my mother had made unfounded accusations against her and they came and took her away.'

Arisa gulped, was quiet a moment, and then spat in the corner angrily. 'No one loves the truth.'

The girl got up and left without looking back. She felt anxious, but the feeling faded when she saw the man. She lay down on her bed and let her eyes fall closed.

She thought about Zahar, Irina's father, a man of love and horror, as Mitka called him, a thin man well over eighty years old. The first time she met him he asked if a man his age should be sent to a camp for cosmopolitanism. Irina had told her that for Zahar the purge of '37 came in 1934. That was when his oldest brother, who had been an official in the Comintern, disappeared.

The train stopped with a strange bark amid cracked asphalt. They had arrived in Suhbaatar, on the Mongolian side of the border. The girl went into the corridor and leaned on the railing. The carriage door opened and a gust of angry wind rushed in followed by a group of passport inspectors in blue uniforms and cute garrison caps who crowded into the carriage reeking of asphalt, followed by sombre border guards, and then the door closed. The border guards dragged the man out of the compartment into the corridor. He opened one eye, which immediately closed again. The back of his shirt was wet.

When another ritual inspection was over, one of the border guards handed the girl the sketchbook that had been confiscated on the Soviet side, an amused smile on his face. Shadows of train carriages crawled across the platform, a lonely yak walked past the window, against the orange glow of the gritty sheets of ice, and the Soviet Union was left behind, the mineral water vending machines (1 kopeck without syrup, 3 kopecks with), the minibus taxis, the girls in braids and black-and-white school dresses, the unknown land, its backwaters and deep basins, its cities built overnight, district centres, villages, bogs, wetlands, forested provinces, woods, wastes, clearcuts, its poorly retouched photos of Politburo members hung around a central plaza, curious people outside the restricted shops, communal saunas, city-centre department stores, street sweepers, snow shovellers, hotel doormen enjoying their bribes, flavourful vodka, dry Georgian champagne, and the feeling of safety on Soviet streets in the wee hours. The filling café food, slogans painted in white on a red background, queues at theatre ticket windows, ice-cream stands and juice cocktails, folk music, currency bar discos and rambunctious young people at one a.m. among dreary rows of suburban prefabs in the middle of a ruined landscape, are left behind. The Soviet Union is left behind, the Lenin statues and portraits, the watercolour paintings of deserted shores on a foam-flecked, stormy sea, the mechanics, oil workers, wretched men working on *kolkhozes,* miners, address and phone-number kiosks, the monuments to the Revolution, the dance pavilions in the parks, the old couples swaying to the beat of a mournful waltz with fur hats on their heads, the stair brooms, entryway brooms, cabin brooms, chamber brooms, cellar brooms, pavement brooms, barn brooms, stable brooms, bathroom brooms, front yard brooms, back yard brooms, garden brooms, well brooms, the old ladies wrapped in big, black cardigans with dusty leggings and threadbare slippers on their feet, lackadaisically swinging their wilted brooms. The casual aggressiveness in the trolley-buses and food shops, in *kolkhoz* cellars, in the dark corners of commune apartments, the gameness, the utopian spirit, the impracticality, the unwillingness to be independent, the self-sacrifice, resignation, constant complaining, legalised loafing, the passive citizenry, whose inventiveness has no bounds. A country where bad luck is interpreted as good luck, left behind. The clocks on the walls in the street lobbies of Moscow's official buildings, telling the time, the cabinets of experts, the factory party committees, secret gambling dens, clandestine home concerts, art exhibits in artists' studios, the local committees, sentry booths, blini booths, biscuit booths, patched roofs, houses collapsed under the snow, the millions of peasants who died of hunger, the city dwellers, the workers, the millions in prisons, the loyal citizens broken down by

work camps and labour sites who died of cold, the denuncia-
tions, the Party tyranny, the choiceless elections, the election
fraud, the grovelling and inordinate mendacity, the millions
fallen in useless wars, the men, women and children executed
at the edges of mass graves, the millions of Soviet citizens
that the machine has abused, tortured, mistreated, neglected,
trampled, cowed, humiliated, oppressed, terrorised, cheated,
raised on violence, made to suffer, are all left behind. The
Soviet Union, a tired, dirty country, is left behind, and the
train plunges into nature, throbs across the sandy, desert landscape. Everything is in motion: snow, water, air, trees, clouds,
wind, cities, villages, people, thoughts.

She thinks about how she's come to love that strange
country, its subservient, anarchistic, obedient, rebellious,
callous, inventive, patient, fatalistic, proud, all-knowing,
hateful, sorrowful, joyful, hopeless, satisfied, submissive,
loving, tough people, content with little. Could she love them
both – Mitka and Irina? A boy and his mother.

The night speeds through the dark into dim morning. The
morning breaks out in a new, lightless day. Snow rises from
the ground up the tree trunks, a hawk perches on an orange
cloud, looking down at the slithering worm of train.

When the confusion died down and the baggage handlers
had settled back into their places, Arisa and Sonechka dragged
the man into the compartment. Arisa cursed to herself. 'The
old goat's as heavy as a gravestone.'

The man rattled and whimpered, an agonised look on his
face. He straightened his back for a moment and stared at the
girl, his gaze unwavering, then collapsed in a heap. His face was
very old and tired. He looked at her again, sleepily, disdainfully.

'Where's my bottle of vodka? Give it to me!'

Arisa looked amused and said in a motherly voice, 'Shut your trap and get your arse to sleep.'

The man sank into restless sleep. His shirt lay open and his sweaty, hairy chest glistened in the dim light of the very early spring morning.

A MELANCHOLY GREY MORNING LIGHT floated into the compartment and illuminated the man's languid face. Gusts of wind buffeted the train. The empty tea glasses gazed at the sleeping man. The girl looked out of the window at an entirely new landscape. In the dim glow of the morning sun, beyond the musical staff of telegraph wires, she saw the first hundred-head herd of colourful horses, the thousands of greasy-tailed sheep with black spots on their foreheads, and she thought of that July day when she came back from her summer vacation in Finland and Mitka was at the station to meet her. She thought about how they had gone to the boarding house, run up the nine flights of stairs hand in hand, how the hallway had been filled knee-high with the fluffy heads of dandelions, how they'd run up and down the hallway like children, the dandelion fluff drifting in and out of the windows.

The train slowed its speed at a spot where a village of yurts came right up to the tracks, and soon slid to a side track to make way for a long column of freight cars. She looked out of the grey window at the yurts. There were five of them, with a yard left in the middle. In the courtyard was a long-shafted wooden cart. Next to it stood a young woman in a traditional red Mongolian dress with a small child in her arms. She had a yellow-flowered scarf wound around her head. The woman glanced in the direction of the train; a little boy behind her struggled onto the back of a skinny-legged foal.

The man stirred in his bed. He tossed restlessly, as if trying to shake off unpleasant memories, then lay with his back to her. His back was covered in tattoos: in the centre the Virgin Mary with the baby Jesus in her arms, on one shoulder a temple with one onion dome and a star.

BY EIGHT O'CLOCK the train was spitting out its passengers at Ulan Bator's Soviet-style railway station. Gritty sleet, mud and snow pattered the train window. She was trying to wake the man. A Mongolian tour guide was standing in the compartment doorway – a small, slimly built, beautiful, tense, indignant man.

'Are you going into Ulan Bator? Do you have a room reserved in the Intourist Hotel? Why are you still on the train? Gather your things and come with me.'

To effect this, he picked up the girl's suitcase and started to leave. The man was still snoring in his bed.

She followed him into the station hall. It was filled with a floating, dreamy silence. An unwelcoming stickiness on the stone floor adhered to the soles of her shoes. Half-rotted food scraps, wrappers, gobs of spit, and dog and bird shit lay all around; the sharp stench seeped into her skin.

They walked to the taxi stand on the parade side of the station. There wasn't a single car there. The tour guide glanced at his Russian wristwatch with irritation and stared fixedly in the direction of the city. The slow sideways drift of snow turned to sleet – gritty, tattered sheets of ice that dropped into the slush like stones. Everything looked grey, limp, drained somehow, a muddy smell of wet earth hovering everywhere.

A taxi arrived, a small metal deer on its hood. The tour guide sat in the front seat and she sat in the spacious rear of the car. The driver was a fat middle-aged man. He was wearing a Russian-style winter overcoat, an extinguished fifth-class

Belomorkanal *papirosa* hanging from his lips, his face scarred and pitted. The car smelled of petrol and old mutton fat.

The road looked like the ones she remembered from the countryside in her childhood. Mud and mire, pothole upon pothole. Whenever they came to a large puddle in the road the driver pressed the accelerator and slammed straight through it, splashing the mud up in an arc onto the people passing by on foot and on various animal conveyances.

It was just a few kilometres from the station to the hotel but the trip took an hour. Every acceleration was followed by a sharp slam on the brakes and another stretch of crawling along at ten kilometres an hour. Now and then the driver came to a complete stop, got out of the car, opened the hood, swore, and took a black steel can out of the trunk, apparently water to pour into the radiator.

The hotel was like any other hotel for Westerners in any other nameless Soviet city. There was a service counter in the lobby, a small, round table next to the high windows, and a sofa for three covered in plastic. Bricks, a cement mixer, bags of plaster, and boards lay in the middle of the floor. Grey construction dust floated over everything.

The tour guide and the receptionist took care of the paperwork while she waited. Finally, the guide asked her to follow him. They climbed the stairs to the top floor. He opened the heavy, pitifully groaning door, and a vast, Soviet-remodelled suite opened before her. A wonderful view of the whole city, all the way to the Gobi Desert, with a spring storm screaming over its sandy hills, was spread outside the window. There were two rooms in the suite. In the living room there was a simple, stylish sofa set, perhaps designed in East Germany, solidly built chairs with Krakow labels on the armrests, and Russian vases on the tables. A large bed filled the bedroom. On the wall facing the bed was a bold reproduction of Repin's painting of Ivan the Terrible after he killed his son. Madness shone in Ivan's eyes; the son looked like a children's Bible picture of Jesus.

The bathroom was spacious, a yellowish fluorescent light sputtered on the ceiling. There was a full-length bathtub, but the plug had been torn off. The shower worked – refreshing cold water came from both taps.

She looked out of the living-room window at the city for a long time. On the left were two thirteen-storey buildings, on the right, a neighbourhood of yurts, and between them a strange conglomeration that reminded her of a Wild West town. Slanted light from the haggard red sun warmed the armchair.

Thoughts galloped through her mind in a tedious circle. The day ended with a frightening sunset, creeping into evening, moonlight illuminating the yards of the yurt villages. The view of the wide sea of desert simmering on the horizon was beautiful, deserted, bleak. She wrapped herself in the down quilt. She thought about Moscow, the last picnic of the autumn with Irina in the English park, where they'd found a garden bench with yellow maple leaves stuck to its wet surface and Irina had called it the Turgenev bench.

The city started to twinkle with faint lights. The lights encroached on a creeping dusk fading into the black of night. A depressing icy darkness squeezed the city small, soundless. She decided she would call the number Irina had given her tomorrow.

A little after eight o'clock someone knocked discreetly on her door. She opened the door and the tour guide was standing there. They went to breakfast together. She ate a Soviet break-fast, he a Mongolian one, which consisted of tea with milk, biscuits that smelled like lamb, and balls of cornmeal. It felt good to sit across from another person. She told him that she'd come to Ulan Bator to see the petroglyphs along the road leading south from the city. He gave her a stern look.

'Westerners aren't allowed to leave the city.'

She offered him some dollars.

'You come here and act like money can buy you anything you want. Our sacred places are not for sale. I've written up an official schedule for you. We can visit the sights of Ulan Bator together and learn about the history of the country. We'll be staying within the city boundary. I'm responsible for your activities.'

He put the dollars in his pocket.

Outside was springlike and warm; the sky was covered in a thick layer of clouds, but the air was still, and no rain was falling. They went to the history museum, the guide always two steps ahead of her. She walked over the slippery waxed museum floor in felt slippers. The guide moved from one glass case to another and spoke in a rote, monotonous tone. In the middle of one verse he raised his voice.

'The Mongolian Empire formed the foundation for the blossoming of the Soviet Union today. They are greatly in our debt. We Mongols conquered Russia in 1242 and Mongol rule lasted two hundred and forty years. We created a working central government in Russia, and well-organised military and tax-collection systems. We built all of the Russian governing institutions that are still operating in the Soviet Union today. We created a bureaucracy whose task was to serve the government, not the people. We broke the back of Russian morality so fundamentally that they still haven't recovered. We drove an atmosphere of mistrust into the Russians' thick skulls. We taught Ivan the Terrible, and he taught Stalin, that the role of the individual is to submit to the group. If an individual makes a mistake, the whole group responds. It's the world's most effective means of governance. Before the reign of the Mongols the Russians didn't even know how to celebrate, they just drunkenly wallowed in pig shit. They learned from us how to enjoy life. The only things Russians invented were unending laziness, cunning, and blatant deceit. The tax structure required a group of Chinese census takers and tax professionals whose efficiency and expertise were already well known at that time. Since Russia was an unsettled and sparsely inhabited country, we decided to use an indirect governing model. In this system, the Russian nobility collected the taxes for the Mongolian khans – they served as our stooges. Later, the high nobility of the Grand Duchy of Moscow appropriated all of our principles and methods of governance without alteration. We rescued Russia from an insidious invasion of Western culture.'

At lunchtime they walked single file to the hotel and after the meal they went back to the history museum. At dinnertime they returned to the hotel again and went to the restaurant, sat across from each other at a table, and didn't speak. After the three courses of dinner, the guide stood up. 'The doors of the hotel close at eight o'clock. After that no one can get in or out. Please follow our rules. For your own good. It would be wise to remember that our laws have no concept of rape.'

At the corner near the hotel a skittish dog with a sticky coat looked at her with frightened eyes. Her mood was becoming more and more desolate. The coldness of the surrounding land, the miserable, damp winds and desert nights were getting under her skin. People shivered with cold. There were two Soviet-style shops across the street, one a delicatessen, the other a stationer's. There was a loudspeaker next to the door of the delicatessen, spewing out a Soviet hit. Shelves nearly empty stared out of the display window. In front of the shop was a cooler filled with a frozen brick of fish and two plastic bags of milk.

In addition to paper products the stationer's also sold Russian black bread, pies filled with lamb, vinegared pickles, and sculpin in tomato sauce.

There was a post office behind the stationer's. On the wall of the post office was a map with the migration routes of sheep marked on it. She wrote a few postcards and bought an extra strip of stamps depicting Mongolian industry.

She dodged the puddles of slush, careening wrecks of chubby old Soviet cars held together with screws, and horses pulling disintegrating carts on the main street. A flock of children dressed in colourful winter clothes played in the courtyard of a three-storey building. The lid of a dustbin was torn off and garbage overflowed onto the dirty ice of the yard. Behind the dustbin she caught a glimpse of the lacerated carcass of a young horse.

She returned to the hotel. She thought about her com-partment companion, what he had said about the Mongols ... how can a nation with such a great history have withered so?

She looked for the number Irina had given her. She called from the hotel telephone for an hour before she got through. A soft, friendly male voice answered. When she'd given him greetings from Irina and explained who she was and why she was in town, he burst into uncontrollable laughter. She even-tually got him to agree to come to the hotel with a friend the next day after dark.

She sat on the sofa again. The late light of a feeble sun shimmered heavy over the roofs of the yurts. She turned on the radio, which was tuned to a Russian-language channel. News, reviews, reports on the national elections, and a little Stravinsky.

The following evening at six o'clock, just as arranged, there was a knock on her door. Two tall, giggling men in their thir-ties stood in the hallway. They sat down shyly on the sofa. She offered them some Black Label whisky. They emptied their glasses in one swallow, she refilled the glasses, and they did it again. They made a promise to show her the real Ulan Bator and the real Mongolia.

At eight o'clock there was a stern knock at the door. Before she had time to get up, the door opened and three sturdy men walked in. Her guests' faces turned suddenly yellow and all five men were gone in an instant. Their steps echoed in the empty hallway. She realised what had just happened and who the three strangers were. She lost all strength in her legs; she felt cold and weak. She tried to go to sleep but sleep wouldn't come. She remembered a January Moscow night.

She and Mitka were standing in front of the Red October metro station cursing because they'd missed the last train. They'd spent a long evening at Arkady's place, a lot of wine and cigarettes. They were cold and had been trying to stop passing cars. Finally a blue Lada stopped. Behind the wheel sat a small dark hairy man who said he would take them home. On the way he asked Mitka if he would like to buy some quality cloud. Soon they were far from home, in some seedy suburb. She and Mitka followed the man into an unfurnished flat. There were a couple of dirty mattresses on the floor, cigarette butts and empty liquor bottles. Mitka made the deal, and just as they were leaving the driver grabbed an axe from behind the door and swung it at Mitka, knocking him unconscious. She didn't have a chance to scream before the man had grabbed her by the neck and was squeezing so hard she couldn't breathe. The man was drinking heavily, and in the wee hours he passed out and Mitka was able to drag himself, covered in blood, into the hallway to call for help.

The girl opened her eyes. There was no sound but the quick beat of her heart and the two-note tick of the clock. She snatched up the clock and put it in her suitcase. She lay awake waiting for sleep to come and free her from herself and her fears. The Mongolian sky was filled with stars; they were bright and near, lighting up the blackness of the sky like summer lightning, but she couldn't see them from under the covers. The hotel was quiet. Ulan Bator was quiet. The silence of the universe was so deep that all she could hear was the hum in her ears. Terror came and went; sometimes she was

filled with fear, then anger, and then something else, something she had to let go of, and finally nothing but a great
regret. The darkness pressed down on her head so hard that
it turned transparent. Finally the harsh night began to lose its
meaning and gradually made way for the weak glimmer of
morning.

She sat impatiently on a sofa in the hotel lobby waiting for
the guide. She wanted to talk to someone about everything
that had happened the evening before. She heard a strange
groan from the direction of the elevator, and when she turned
to look, she saw the same three security service workers. They
were dragging her guests, beaten unconscious, bruised beyond
recognition, across the lobby towards a Lada that waited
outside. Blood and dirt smeared over the construction dust
on the marble floor. One of the security men glared at her,
another grimaced, the third didn't even look at her. The hotel
receptionist continued flipping through papers behind the
desk and didn't see anything.

When the yellow Lada had disappeared into the bright
Mongolian morning, a Mongol granny wrapped in a big black
woollen coat and carrying a Latvian tin bucket came up from
the basement, cleaned the floor, and went back downstairs.

At breakfast she told the guide about her guests and how
they were taken away and what she had just seen.

When she had finished, the guide smiled drily and said he
didn't want to hear about the matter again.

They spent a silent day at the natural history museum.

The next morning she walked behind her guide through the

city and thought about Irina, but Irina seemed to have slipped into the distance somewhere. When they passed the state telephone office she told the guide she wanted to call Moscow. He tried to prevent her, but she went inside and ordered ten minutes on the phone, in a panic. They waited there for six hours, the guide staring at the floor angrily, before the operator announced that Irina wasn't answering. Of course she wasn't – Irina and Mitka were still in the south.

Late that night a fierce wind blew up. It tore at the tin roof of the hotel and sent oil barrels tumbling down the ice-covered streets. The hotel shook in the buffeting wind, creaked, cracked, felt like it would come falling down. The girl was cold. The windstorm was followed by a blizzard of gritty snow from the desert that whipped straight at the hotel windows and melted against the warm panes of glass. She imagined it turning the screws in the window frames, the bolts falling out, nails breaking in two, the cement crumbling, the whole building tilting and collapsing in a heap of sand.

In the morning she told the receptionist that she was sick and didn't need her guide, planned to spend the day in her room resting.

She stood at the window. The indifferent sun moved past from east to west. As evening fell, the sun dropped behind the yurt village and a drear, heavy darkness settled over the city, day changed to evening, evening to night. She watched a satellite that looked like the moon shining hysterically bright over the roofs of the yurts. She missed Moscow and its summer poplars.

She decided to go out and look for the man. She couldn't

think of anything else to do. The night was bright and cold. She left at a run, glancing behind her as she ran, the green beam of a floodlight throwing itself over the hotel, the grey clouds shuttling their way north. She jumped onto the first bus and rode it out of the city. Lanterns from distant yurt villages flickered in the darkness. The bus passed a group of colourless people walking next to the road, swaying randomly. Some of them had sacks on their backs, some had their arms full of packages and other burdens. The bus veered towards a new building site where half-finished Soviet-style highrises languished. The buildings stood with their bellies open in the middle of the torn-up, ravaged ground. Scaffolding rose up on every side – beams, stairways, floors, canopies, hallways, bridges. Faint lights from a village of builders' barracks greeted the coming night. An old truck and a battered bulldozer lay collapsed outside the fence. Ruddy rings of lampposts drew trembling ellipses on the black sky, the scaffolds lit with the yellow illumination of evening.

She walked along a half-built road. The ruts left by the trucks were filled with watery sludge. Swinging lanterns clinked against metal wires at the gate to the guards' barracks, where a Komsomolets excavator stood out at the front like a guard dog, a one-legged Lapp chickadee hopping along its roof. She knocked on the barracks door for a long time before the sleepy watchman came to open it. Stuffy heat wafted out of the barracks onto her face. The watchman asked in a stern voice what she wanted. He looked at her with his head to one side and smiled.

'I've always wondered what young women like you see in that old phoney. The more lost the cause the more interesting

it is. You women have no sense of self-preservation. Vadim
Nikolayevich Ivanov is staying over there in the barracks, but
you can't go there. Give me your number. He'll call you if he
wants to.'

She handed him the hotel address and her room number.

'Don't forget – I warned you.'

She went back to the hotel, past the nauseating stench
of poisoned yurt slums, through the red dark of night, the
dismal, frozen silence. All the stars of Orion shone straight
down on her, and the snowy moon rose slowly into the sky
from behind a concrete wall. Much later a deaf dawn appeared
in the east and lit up the low-hanging clouds. A few flakes of
snow drifted onto her fevered face.

Before she fell asleep she listened to the progress of the
waking morning. She thought about Siberia's frosty, spent
forests, spread like a wall along the edge of a sea of fields.
She thought of the blizzarded, stiff-frozen borderlands, where
herds of reindeer wandered aimlessly, lazily looking for food,
the impenetrable wilderness, puny hills, uninhabited provinces, snowstorms, swarms of mosquitoes, and autumn's still,
misty damp wrapping itself around a little village.

He didn't call.

The next day she went with the tour guide to Suhbaatar's
mausoleum, Bogd Khan's winter palace, and the Lenin statue.
When they ran out of sights, she tried one more time. She
reminded the guide about the petroglyphs. He laughed with
amusement and she understood that there was no point in
bringing it up again. She looked out of the grey hotel window
at the quiet clouds crawling unhurried to the east.

When Mitka came home after eight months of psychiatric treatment, she sensed that he had guessed everything. Irina had arranged through her office for herself and Mitka to stay in a citizens' sanatorium in the Crimea. The purpose was for them to rest, and if his reason returned to its former sharpness, everything would be just as it was before. Irina had prepared her for this, for the fact that it might be as if nothing had happened while he was away.

Mornings crawled into days, days into evenings, deep nights filled the earth and sky, as long as the life to come, filled with a hum, with the hiss of radiators, the cold dryness of sheets, the dry rustle of gritty snowfall. She paced around her room, looked out of the window at the sleeping city, the greasy, struggling wind sinking into the darkness of the city. She gazed at the nights, the stars coming out so large and pale she could have touched them. She waited for the mornings, the stars twinkling uncertainly for a moment and disappearing. She watched the slow rise and set of the desperate sun, the momentary light of falling stars, and cursed herself. She was tired and empty. Far away from everything. Even herself.

Gradually, she accepted her solitude and stopped waiting for him to call. She began to bear the continual anxiety, the growing pressure, the pain in her chest, a little better. She learned to listen a little more calmly to her own tense breathing and the restless beat of her overwrought heart devouring her blood.

One evening he came. He smelled of mare's milk *kumis* and mutton fat. She sobbed. As they stepped outside, a rock-hard, heavy southwest wind shoved them along, carrying them towards a yurt suburb. He took hold of her shoulder and pulled her next to him, fatherly. She told him what had happened. She was crying, but the wind from beyond the yurts dried her tears so quickly that he didn't see them. He listened to her without interrupting, and when she came to the end of the story, he burst into boisterous laughter.

'You really are stupid. I've never met a broad like you, and I've come across all kinds. Don't worry. It'll all work out.'

He swallowed his laughter. He scratched the back of his head and snarled. 'I wonder what those guys had been up to, for God to punish them like that? The law here barely recognises manslaughter, fines you about as much as the price of a bottle of black-market vodka. They must be quite the rascals, eh?'

They walked on in silence. A gust of air blasted around a corner, she swallowed it and coughed.

'When things don't get better, they get worse, and it's a short road from bad to good. Don't worry, my girl, a bit of bad luck can suddenly change to a bit of good. Those bums got what they asked for. No normal Mongolian man goes to a hotel to meet a Western tourist – it's like suicide.'

He looked at her pityingly.

'I once had a whore here who I really liked a lot. She had a six-year-old son who always gave me a murderous stare. When I was screwing her I was always afraid he could come up behind me and put a Finnish pen through my skull. I bought him a set of building blocks from Moscow, the kind you can use to build all of Red Square, with the church and Lenin's mausoleum. When I gave it to him, he threw it in the corner and stared at me like he could have killed me. But when I went to get some pussy later on, the whore told me to look under the bed. There was Red Square in all its glory, handsome as Beria's dick.'

She jumped over a pile of horse manure in front of a drinks machine and laughed. There was a snowy amusement park behind a low warehouse where a tired old ferris wheel moped, stiff with cold. He took off, running towards the park. She watched as he slipped through the hanging half-open door of the leaning, abandoned booth and, as if by magic, the light bulbs strung around the park flickered on in faint tatters of light and the ferris wheel creaked into motion, first rattling slowly, then growing faster with a steady whine. She looked first at the man, then at the ferris wheel, then at the outlandish city with its wind-licked, blackened, discarded remains of yurts, strewn over a wasteland. The melting snow smelled like spring. A puddle of greasy black liquid spread from an oil barrel thrown into a snow drift. She thought about Moscow, Malaya Nikitskaya, where she and Irina once walked, the yellow lights gliding through the autumn fog.

The darkness thickened to a blue mist over the amusement park. He walked her back to the hotel. They could see from a distance a gigantic puddle of oily sludge, a cold red circle of moon shining on its surface. Little children were playing at the edge of the puddle, although it was night. A girl barely four years old, her legs swollen, was gathering oil in a broken bottle. A boy younger than her was wading in the puddle, shoeless, splashing it on himself.

The hotel was locked. The two of them stood with their backs to the wind and waited. The faint light of the moon shone on the puddles of slush, an indifferent wind whistled around the building. A sullen functionary eventually came and opened the door. The man followed her to the desk in the lobby and handed her a twenty-five-rouble note. She smiled bashfully back at him. He winked at her and left.

The girl climbed the stairs to her room and collapsed happily onto the sofa. She fell asleep with all her clothes on, at peace, thinking of nothing.

A HALF MOON STILL HUNG over the yurts despite the concentrated sunlight. Small white clouds scuttled briskly across the lid of sky. Columns of trucks rumbled towards construction sites, shaking the window of her room, horses whinnied and flicked away the burning rays of sun with their long thick tails, old men in lambskin coats puffed cigarettes on the main street in front of the department store, women hurried by carrying milk pails.

When she went down to the lobby, the man handed her a budding cyclamen and kissed her three times on the cheeks.

'Is this the fellow that's been bothering you?'

He pointed disdainfully at the tour guide. When she nodded, he took the man aside. A moment later the guide left without looking back, angry and humiliated, but well paid.

'We won't have any more trouble from that louse,' he said with a laugh. 'Walking around in rags, but still full of himself.'

A shiny old Volga was waiting for them outside behind a buzzing telegraph pole, its thin, goateed driver dangling an extinguished cigarette in a short amber holder.

'This here's Gafur, soldier of the Golden Horde and my friend at the construction site. A real Tatar. Not one of these Swabian Protestants. Do you know what kind of fellows these Tatars are? They gave Hitler a gilded saddle as a present, and to repay them Stalin killed the whole nation, millions of them. Gafur's the only one left alive.'

Gafur laughed. The man got in the front beside him, the girl in the back. The car smelled of sweat and dandruff.

'Complete dashboard with frame-suspended pedals, four on the column, and built-in radio. And best of all, with very little money you get lots of little extra annoyances.'

Gafur started the engine with a quick sharp movement of his hand, stomped on the accelerator so hard that the back wheels skidded in the slippery slush, and edged the nose of the car out of the driveway, revving it for all it was worth. The retreating road was covered in a thick layer of dust mixed with sand and snow. Gafur said he'd been with his Tatyana for fifteen years and successfully driven her from Alma Ata to Mongolia.

Now and then the car bounced over to the right side of the road, then the left. Oncoming trucks rushed by on one side or the other. Gafur suddenly slammed on the brakes, causing the man to hit his head on the windshield, then immediately floored the accelerator so that the girl was slammed against the back headrest. The man pointed towards the Golden Mountains on the horizon, brightly painted with sunshine. They glowed red in some places, white in others.

'Let's head for the mountains. Some country air and nature will do us good. I'll sell you to some horse herder who'll screw your brains out and make you the best goat milker in Mongolia.'

Here and there trucks idled with steaming water shooting out of them. There were sheep and goats of different colours everywhere. A caravan of camels with full loads undulated in the distance. One of the camels had a gigantic antenna contraption on its back. The Volga lurched and coughed as it roared along, the radio rasping. The black-spotted sun shed its hot rays through the rear window; the girl let her cheek press up against the cool glass.

She came awake with a hard knock. The car had stopped in the middle of a clear-running river. Gafur cursed and the man laughed.

The two men took off their shoes, socks, and trousers, and asked her to get behind the wheel while the engine continued to knock, wheeze and sputter. They got behind the car and pushed. She wrenched the transmission into first, gently lifted her foot from the clutch, and pressed the accelerator to the floor. The men shivered in the ice-cold water all the way across the river. Luckily the water was shallow, only knee-deep. She got to the other side and got out of the car.

'I'll tame you yet, you whore,' Gafur hissed, hopping back in and furiously seizing the steering wheel.

The man looked at Gafur and wrinkled his brow. Gafur punched the car straight into second gear, stomped vehemently on the accelerator, and cranked the wheel farther than was reasonable. The Volga flung itself from the slippery bank onto level ground. Feodor Challiapin sang from the hefty vacuum-tube radio built into the dashboard.

The road ascended into the mountains. The Volga jerked its way up the steep, narrow route. The fiery red sun hung at the edge of the snow-covered sandy steppe and started to set; a pink mist hovered low over the desert. Owls appeared, loitering in the middle of the road and flapping into flight just as the Volga was about to crush them. Sometimes the car stopped and the girl got behind the wheel as the men pushed. Sometimes they stopped along the road to let the engine cool.

It was a steep climb and the car's strong but simple engine couldn't go more than a few metres at a time. The girl and the man walked alongside the car. She took very careful sips of the thin mountain air. A melancholy night lit by a hazy blue moon loomed far beyond the mountains and spread peacefully around them. At midnight the Volga started to whine, then to howl.

'Squealing like a sow,' Gafur growled in a wounded voice, just as the engine died completely.

He opened the hood. The large-celled radiator leered at him from its loose corner to the left of the engine, hot as fire, the coolant grid hanging sadly, almost touching the ground. The two men stared at the engine for a long time, but neither of them touched it.

Gafur gazed in disbelief at the engine, then at the man. The man sat down on a large stone, watched a hawk gliding above them along the restless bird's trail of the Milky Way crackling atop the nearest mountain. He lit a cigarette and smoked it slowly, calmly blowing smoke.

'I once got so mad at Katinka that I took a sledgehammer to her washing machine. Katinka gathered her things and she and her boy took off to her mother's house in Leningrad. They would have stayed there, too, but I went and got them three months later. A man can't get along without a woman. Even if he can find some pussy, he'll still need somebody to make the soup.'

He lifted a hand to his temple and looked like a cockroach sitting there.

The waxing moon hovered over the mountainside; the landscape of sand mixed with snow spread deathlike, tranquil, silent.

They gently rolled the car to the side of the road and Gafur stroked its sickly chassis. He was humming contentedly

– apparently he and the Volga had made up. The man slumped into the back seat and pulled his cap over his eyes. The girl leaned against an enormous boulder. The fat moon and glaring stars lit up the roadside, and the cold, naked rocks pressed in at either side of the mountain road. A pale mist snaked through the ravines and a few yaks huddled in the valley, while over the mountains an opaque, tired sky billowed, covered in snowclouds.

The girl touched the surface of the boulder with her hand and felt a gouge cut in it. She looked at it more closely. The headlights of a swaying truck went past, brushing over the stone. There were deer, goats, and other animals in various poses painted on its surface. She waited for the flash of lights from the next truck. She moved her fingers slowly over the surface of the rock. There were marks carved around the animals. Tree signs, Uigur signs, runes. She laid her cheek against the boulder and kissed it, and tears ran down her cheeks.

Gafur appeared beside her. He took a Kazbek out of his pocket and started to smoke. Unfriendly mud splashed in the puddles as half-ton trucks splattered with mire and battered by rocks and potholes roared and rattled past in an almost continuous line, leaving ruts in the soft roadway. They were like ravines in the slippery, overflowing mud. The girl stroked the rock surreptitiously. Gafur smoked his cigarette and threw the stub on the ground.

'It was a warm summer morning in Kazan. I was sitting on the bench behind our building smoking some hash. I watched clouds shaped like grand pianos flitting across the brilliant sky and I thought, soon I'll be flying above them. Then I heard a horrible boom and a pressure wave slammed me all the way to the back of the yard. When I lifted my head a few hours later I saw that the whole building had collapsed. Grey dust and smoke covered everything, and when I looked at the sky I saw a black starlit August night.'

She listened, as she had become used to doing.

'I'm a free man. I live in the here and now. I focus on what I like, and let everything else alone. I watch from the sidelines and live like the animals do. That's the way I am. So if the young lady is in the mood for a shot of heroin made from first-class, professionally cultivated Afghan opium, uncle's got some in his pocket.'

A plump, poison-green cloud sailed alone across the sky. Soon it had settled in front of the moon and smothered its gleaming light. The girl felt the glow of the petroglyph under her hand. Gafur took a spoon and a small bag of white powder out of his pocket, prepared his fix, lifted his wide-cut trouser-leg and jabbed the needle somewhere into his shin, with an apparently practised aim.

'Now the goodness is pumping into every vein and brain cell,' he whispered languidly.

A new star appeared in the sky, a meteor fell, beams of star-light splashed across the pitch-blackness, the planets glowed. She brushed her fingers against the distant past once more and felt the power of life within her. They walked to the car. The air was opaque now, like a thin glue. She got in the back seat, the man moved to the front, and Gafur got behind the wheel. Watery mud flew into the windshield. White sleet fell from the sky and soon it had covered the smudges of dirt, then the whole windshield. They were freezing in the cold car but the man soon drew forth a large green bottle. It was filled with spiked *kumis.* He pulled a long baguette and three dirty glasses from under the front seat.

'These formerly fierce horsemen were the toughest working men in Khabarovsk and Novosibirsk a couple of decades ago, way ahead of us Russians. Things are different now. Gafur sits tight on his needle, ready to sell the blood out of his veins if need be to get his next dose. And so, dear comrades, my beloved homeland grows more beautiful year after year, but never blossoms. Winter's gone; summer's here; let us lift our glasses to friendship, with or without the needle.'

As soon as a little light penetrated the muddy windshield, the girl snapped awake from her stupor. She carefully opened the creaking door and eased out of the car. A gentle whirlwind brushed her sleepy face and brought with it the earthy smell of early spring. High in the sky a white dinosaur bounded brightly.

Gafur poured oil into the engine, hoping it would forgive him and love him again. The car pinged good-naturedly and started up. Bright rays of early morning sunshine cut across the sky. The man put on his sunglasses. Gafur kept squeezing the steering wheel nervously, although he'd already had his morning fix, and accelerated the Volga. The car leapt onto the road.

The full sun threw its first rays over the numb and sleeping sandy steppe. Soon it billowed yellow and made the snow-streaked mountains sparkle gold. Sunbeams moved along the mountainsides, the steep narrow road, and the ice-hard drifts glittering with powdery snow. For a moment everything stopped, then the sleepy sky exploded. Hail the size of ping-pong balls came zinging down.

Three yurts flitted into view from beyond a curve in the twisting road. They stood on a broad low place near a river. Snakes of smoke wriggled from them towards the pulsating sky. Everywhere she looked lay the bodies of frozen dead animals. A Mongolian ass swollen like a ball, the pecked eyes of yaks, hundreds of carcasses of spotted sheep and delicate goats. The winter's storms had hardened the snow.

'*Golod i holod*,' the man grunted mournfully. 'We're here, my girl! More than three kilometres up. A secret, stinking little world. Don't piss in running water around here. If you do, you'll die.'

Gafur drove the car behind a yurt and turned off the engine. The village children formed a circle around the Volga. They stared at the girl in disbelief, afraid.

She watched a lone scrap of red fabric as the wind blew it up the mountainside. It got stuck briefly on a pine branch, then on a sharp piece of stone, dived into a sheltered hollow for a moment, then continued its journey up to the uninhabited and unexplored rocky, rugged heights. Frightened, half-wild, restlessly twitching Gobi horses snorted beside one of the yurts. They had small heads, narrow ears and graceful legs, and halters of braided leather on short ropes tied loosely to a clothesline. Thus tied they could move like dogs leashed to a cable. A full-grown tundra falcon was perched on a wooden rail next to the door of the yurt. One of its legs was tied to the rail with a strip of reindeer hide.

Boulders mounded with snow rose high on either side of the village. The golden heights of the mountains were close; the air smelled of pungent herbs, water babbled in the stream. In the distance behind the yurts a herd of horses wandered.

One of the horses was so white that it nearly disappeared as it galloped over the snowy pasture. Beyond the horses a flock of goats lounged in the mellow sunshine.

The girl's head hurt; she didn't feel well. The man gave her a pill. A few brisk, curious women came out of a yurt, a man with a slack yellow face, black-browed eyes, and green spots on his forehead appeared from behind it. He greeted the men with familiarity. He didn't greet the girl, just looked at her for a long time. A little later he gestured towards the yurt – the women were to bring her inside to rest.

'Don't step on the threshold when you go in. If you do, they'll chop your head off,' the man said, cracking his knuckles.

The women walked in front of her and opened the door. It was painted red and squeaked pathetically. She stepped inside warily. In the middle of the yurt a small fire smoked on the bare ground, a young woman and an old woman bustling around it. When they noticed her through the curtain of smoke they motioned for her to sit near the fire. The older woman handed her a bowl of white tea.

Soon the young woman spread a flowered mattress on the floor – the guest bed. The older woman laid a neatly folded cotton quilt over it and placed a large cushion at one end. They gave her a thick lambskin for a blanket. She looked at the flowered fabric covering the walls, the skilfully made, bright-coloured rugs on the floor, the hand-painted dishes and little cloth dolls hanging from the ceiling and lying on top of a blue Chinese cabinet, and soon fell asleep.

She woke to the hideous shriek of a song thrush. She watched from her mattress as Gafur and the people of the yurt gnawed at mutton, without greed or any great gusto, and gulped down *kumis*. She was careful not to step on the threshold when she went outside. The gentle silence of the night greeted her. The seething sun had set behind the Golden Mountains and the sky gradually was lit with a thousand dry, restless stars. They swept across the blue space, the Milky Way zigzagging fitfully above the mountains, galaxies hissing over the village of yurts. She sat down on a stone, touched its cold surface. The stone was silent. She watched the song thrush torment the tethered falcon.

In the morning her eyes hurt again. Her head was splitting; there was an unbearable cosmic roar in her ears. Her shoulders slumped, her head hung limply.

The bright icy sun didn't ask forgiveness. In the summer, that same sun dried up the raindrops before they could reach the earth. A stinging icy wind flowed from the north, dragging a mountain crow and a tattered burlap sack with it. Frost laid down by the night's freeze grew from the ground up the walls of the yurt. Thin black trails of smoke floated sleepily through the air.

The girl stood still. From the east a piercing brightness came, in the west a thick grey gelatinous fog swirled, and in the north, at the northern edge of the sky, hung a blood-red comet. It looked like an old 1930s decal glued to a paper sky stained with dark-blue ink. She marvelled at a flock of cranes that stepped in a phalanx along the level ground, pecking up dead grasshoppers from the autumn before. She saw five black long-haired bulls. They were scraping the ice with their hooves to find the grass beneath. She heard the goats bleating and strolled towards a grove of frosty, sad-hanging branches. The women were milking the goats.

Gafur appeared out of nowhere, lively, enjoying his fix, capering over the hard-frozen snow in his dandy's pointy-toed shoes, and followed a Mongolian man to where the horses were. They took the harnesses of two restive horses and led them out in front of the yurt. They were on their way to look for a half-tamed flock of sheep that had disappeared during the night.

She walked to the edge of the bubbling river. From there she could see the wooden fence of the corral, which was empty now. A small mongrel dog followed her. White steam rose from its mouth. It stopped to watch her, thought for a moment, stared at her with bitter green eyes, then crept up to where she stood, laid its snout against her knee, sighed deeply, and continued on its way. Farther up the mountain a thick-furred camel swayed, pulling a flimsy long-shafted cart behind it. The man saw the girl. He walked over to her.

'You can't see farther than your nose, no matter how you try. But remember, even at the darkest moments, beyond the dead horizon, there's always life. When Mishka left, I envied him. He got away and I stayed behind. But now …'

He smelled like warm sweat. The strong sunlight reflected from the frozen mountainside where powdered snow had fallen during the night. A light, melancholy feeling floated like a low cloud over the pure landscape. He scratched the back of his head thoughtfully. The sky glowed with spring light.

'Do you know why people live longer than other animals do? It's because animals live by their instincts, and they don't make mistakes. We people, on the other hand, rely on reason, and we screw up all the time. We spend half our lives messing things up, half realising the stupid mistakes we've made, and the rest of the time trying to fix whatever we can. We need all the years we live for all that rigamarole. I was born in 1941. My father, whom I didn't get to choose, begat me on his way from the work camp to the front. My mother is a mean, bitter woman. She hated my father for travelling in a prison carriage to get to a soup kettle in Siberia, leaving her to be trampled by the war and starve. I knew everything about life when I was five, and I spent the next forty years trying to understand it.'

He picked up a handful of rocks and started to toss them into the water. She could see his hands growing hard.

'I often wonder at how I've managed to stay alive. When I was young I was crazy with fear, then I learned to overcome fear. I studied judo and five years later I was a black belt. After that I wasn't afraid. I'm ready to die at any time. I still get goosebumps when I go home to Moscow and hear my mother breathing in the next room. I despise my mother; sometimes I feel sorry for her. A person who's always right is a blind, deaf murderer. But you wouldn't understand that, and you don't have to. As long as you're here.'

He stopped speaking and a smothered silence settled around them. He took his knife out of his boot, sprang its sharp blade open, and felt it with a finger, its brightly polished surface. Disappointment lay deep in his half-closed eyes.

'I didn't have a family, or relationships. That thread broke before I was born, and why wake the ghosts of the past? The cart of the past only leads to the rubbish dump.' He held the knife out to her. 'This is my father's cross, a Siberian knife. I don't know all he did with it, but I stabbed Vimma with this knife. One good-for-nothing killing another.'

He touched his cheek with the blade. 'It's yours now.'

She took the knife. It was heavy. The black handle was made of bone and had a silver Orthodox cross inlaid in it. She felt the power of the knife, and the trip up to this point, with all its light and shadow, flooded through her. Its joys, sorrows, hope, hopelessness, hate and, perhaps, love. Then she looked him in the eye and said, as Job said: 'For the thing which I greatly feared is come upon me, and that which I was afraid of is come to me, Vadim Nikolayevich.'

He touched her hand tenderly, took a pack of *papirosas* out of his pocket, and lit one. She snapped the blade open and looked at the man's hands. She looked at the heavy sharp knife. How many people had been killed with it?

She dug in her pocket, took out a twenty-five-rouble note, and handed it to him. He took the note, smiling faintly, and folded it into his pocket. The thick snow squeaked under his heavy leather shoes. Tatters of large light snowflakes drifted from the sky.

When he left, the children came. They admired and begged for everything she had on: a ring, a necklace, buttons, a belt, hairpins, her scarf. She handed her necklace to the oldest boy. He looked at it for a moment, threw it on the ground, and started to beg for her shoes. Black-tailed squirrels followed after the children. They jumped onto her shoulders and head; one tried to nibble at her face. The children swarmed around her and sicced the squirrels on her. One small boy had a stick in his hand and he tried to poke her with it. When she screamed loudly he dashed away, but he soon came back and continued to poke her. She grabbed the stick from his hand and broke it in two. The boy started to bawl, the squirrels disappeared, and the other children laughed.

She went walking along the shore of the river. The children followed her every step; one of them was throwing small stones at her. The women watched the children and chuckled proudly. The girl put her hand in her pocket and felt the knife; she didn't think about the children or the women.

The sleepy sky darkened quickly and a strong wind from the mountains threw down a brief shower of grainy snow. Then the wind calmed and the peace of a spring night settled over everything.

Dusk hung lightly over the village as the Mongolian man and Gafur returned from the mountain with the flock of sheep. The Mongolian slaughtered one large sheep, let it bleed from the neck into a red plastic bucket, and handed the bucket to the old woman. She disappeared with it into a yurt.

The Mongolian man flayed the sheep and he and Gafur cut up the meat. Meanwhile the women lit a fire on a stove in the yard. When the meat was cut up, the man put the pieces in the bloody sheepskin, and he and Gafur dragged the bundle over to the stove.

The man opened the stove lid. It was full of hot rocks. He picked up a pair of tongs, lifted the stones one by one off the stove, and put them inside the sheepskin. Then he and Gafur hung the whole thing over the fire to burn the wool from the skin.

An hour later they opened the skin and lifted the cooked meat into a metal dish. A cold wind was rising from the northwest.

The girl went into the yurt to warm herself. The man was sitting at a low table, relaxed, twirling a teaspoon in a glass. She rubbed her hands together over the open fire.

'It'll be May soon, my girl,' he said. 'I like April, but I hate May in Siberia. The wind starts to blow from rotten places, and it brings horrible blizzards with it. It feels obscene and disgusting.'

The limp sun melted from the sky and the moon rose. They sat on the floor of the yurt, each of them in their place. The man handed the host a hand auger, marmalade, a jar of pickles, and a pile of newspapers as a gift, and for the hostess some Polish perfume and amber beads. In return he received fifteen fresh marmot skins. They ate the good mutton in the warmth of the yurt and raised their glasses. Gafur filled a water pipe with marijuana grown in Astrahan and some *neftyanka* made from Khazakstani hemp, strong and oily. The men smoked – it wasn't offered to the women.

It was quiet. A young woman poured *kumis* into mugs.

As evening fell, Gafur and the man got up to leave. They made their long goodbyes to the old man and the women, gave out a few more gifts, and finally went outside. She followed them. Gusty winds tossed fine icy snow through the air. There was a turquoise ring around the grey moon.

The travellers got into the car, the men in front, the girl in the back as before. The car started, huffing and banging. A flock of children ran after it, throwing stones.

The whirling snowstorm and dark of early evening gradually aged into night over the ancient mountains, and made the girl's thoughts return to Moscow. She thought about those Moscow mornings when thick fog covered both shores of the Moscow River, how the fresh, ice-cold water trickled through the fog, the metro trains full of people, country people getting their enormous bags stuck in the metro doors, confused by the escalators, pushing and crowding and dashing around, the mass of passengers drifting from one tunnel to the next. She forgot everything else for a moment. A sandstorm from the north lashed lazily at the windshield.

They got back to the city after midnight.

THEY STOOD FOR A MOMENT in front of the hotel, the two men smoking farewell cigarettes. The man looked at her sharply with his bright eyes, peering from under his brows in the eastern manner, a serious yet boyish look of excitement on his face.

'We're going out goating, going to get a smell of life and death,' he said, waving a hand faintly at her as he went.

The girl sat in her dark room until morning. She thought about Mitka, about the time they were on their way back from Irina's friend's dacha. They'd sat in a crowded electric train that smelled of want and apathy. She'd leaned against Mitka's shoulder and felt motion, the motion of everything around her and the motion inside her. She'd fallen asleep and Mitka had woken her at Moscow station, asked her to name an eighteen-digit number. She said a number and it took only a moment for him to name its fifth root. He practised logarithms with great enthusiasm, the numbers sometimes growing so large in his head that they gave him a fever.

Not until the east was painted in blue light and the stars yellowed to mandarin behind a veil of clouds did the first tears streak down her cheeks.

The tour guide was waiting for her at the restaurant door at breakfast. They ate in silence. The guide looked at her nonchalantly and suggested that she spend her last day in Ulan Bator on her own – he had a German tourist coming.

All day long, a silent snow fell. A gentle wind swept the snow into the potholes to cover the frozen, muddy water.

All that was grey and dull had disappeared. She stepped into a café. Amid the everyday stench and the smell of roasted mutton a primus stove whistled, children wrestled in the slush on the floor, a schoolboy caught the light on the windowsill in a piece of mirror, and she drank a cup of tea with goat's milk.

In the evening she went back to the hotel, packed her few things, put her airline tickets on the bedside table, and focused on breathing. A pleasant gloom searched its way towards her, then reached her. A dim orange star dangling in a crescent moon. The pair of them couldn't quite light up the sleeping town. The stars had fallen frozen into the red sand of the Gobi Desert. Only Venus twinkled in the sky, bright and blazing. The last snowflakes drifted to the ground. She was ready to meet her life, its happiness and unhappiness.

She was ready to go back to Moscow! To Moscow!

# THANKS

Riikka Ala-Harja, Jonni Aromaa, Mihail Berg, Jelena Bonner, Vladimir Dudintsev, Viktor Erofeyev, Venedikt Erofeyev, J. K. Ihalainen, Ilf and Petrov, Anne Kaihua, Risto Kautto, Mihail Lermontov, Nikolai Leskov, Sari Lindstén, Jukka Mallinen, Nadežda Mandelstam, Pekka Mustonen, Vladimir Nabokov, Eila Niaska, Teija Oikkonen, Sofi Oksanen, Outi Parikka, Konstantin Paustovsky, Viktor Pelevin, Paula Pesonen, Pekka Pesonen, Lyudmila Petrushevskaya, Andrei Platonov, Yevgeni Popov, Nina Sadur, Varlam Salamov, Esa Seppänen, Vasili Shukshin, Konstantin Simonov, Andrei Sinyavsky, Vladimir Sorokin, Marina Tarkovskaya, Andrei Tarkovsky, Tatyana Tolstaya, Leo Tolstoy, Artemi Troitski, Yury Trifonov, Marina Tsvetaeva, Ivan Turgenev, Lyudmila Ulitskaya, Jarmo Valtanen, Galina Vishnevskaya, Marina Vlady, Sergei Yesenin, Mihail Zoshchenko, and many others

# WORLD LITERATURE from SERPENT'S TAIL

### THE BOOK OF DISQUIET
Fernando Pessoa

'The very book to read when you wake at 3am and can't get back to sleep – mysteries, misgivings, fears and dreams and wonderment. Like nothing else' Phillip Pullman

ISBN 978 184668 7358
eISBN 978 184765 2379

### DOÑA FLOR AND HER TWO HUSBANDS
Jorge Amado

'A master storyteller' *TLS*

ISBN 978 185242 7108

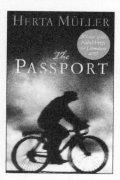

### THE PASSPORT
Herta Müller

Winner of the Nobel Prize for Literature

ISBN 978 185242 1397
eISBN 978 184765 2492

**www.serpentstail.com**
**twitter: @serpentstail**

# WORLD LITERATURE from SERPENT'S TAIL

## THE PIANO TEACHER
### Elfriede Jelinek

Winner of the Nobel Prize for Literature, and a major film by Michael Haneke

ISBN 978 184668 7372
eISBN 978 184765 3062

## HER PRIVATES WE
### Frederic Manning

'[I read *Her Privates We*] every year to remember how things really were so that I will never lie to myself or anyone else about them'
Ernest Hemingway

ISBN 978 184668 7877
eISBN 978 184765 7640

## NO MAN'S LAND
### Edited by Pete Ayrton

The first international collection of First World War fiction by contemporary writers

ISBN 978 184668 9253
eISBN 978 184765 9224

www.serpentstail.com
twitter: @serpentstail

# WORLD LITERATURE from SERPENT'S TAIL

## TOMORROW I'LL BE TWENTY
Alain Mabanckou

'Irreverent wit and madcap energy' Giles Foden, author of *The Last King of Scotland*

ISBN 978 184668 5842
eISBN 978 184765 7893

## MOOD INDIGO
Boris Vian

French cult classic is now a film by Michel Gondry

ISBN 978 184668 9444
eISBN 978 184765 9699

www.serpentstail.com
twitter: @serpentstail